A blush heated her face and she turned abruptly away from him to face the evening beyond the balcony.

She wanted to… She needed… Images of what she wanted came to her. Hot. Clawing. Sweaty. Impossible. She squeezed her eyes shut, pressed a hand over her racing heart. Seven stood just behind her, but she couldn't face him yet. He could easily see the hunger in her face. See how effortless it would be for her to forget her precious principles and make love with him tonight.

"If it makes you feel better, you can tell yourself that kiss was to seal our new business arrangement." His breath brushed the back of her neck. "I'll see you in your office on Monday."

A hot tremor quaked her thighs. She fought it and straightened, then turned around, determined to reclaim her composure and get back on even footing with Seven. But, except for the whispering girls and the woman smoking her cigar, Bailey was alone. She swallowed her disappointment. Then turned back to the night, hoping it would soothe her riotous mind and overheated body.

Books by Lindsay Evans

Harlequin Kimani Romance

Pleasure Under the Sun

LINDSAY EVANS

is a traveler, lover of food and avid café loafer. She's been reading romances since she was a very young girl and feels touched by a certain amount of surreal magic in that she now gets to write her own love stories. *Pleasure Under the Sun* is her debut title for the Harlequin Kimani Romance line.

PLEASURE UNDER THE SUN

LINDSAY EVANS

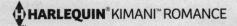
HARLEQUIN® KIMANI™ ROMANCE

For Dorothy Lindsay and Cherie Evans Lyon.
Your encouragement and love lift me up, always.

Recycling programs
for this product may
not exist in your area.

ISBN-13: 978-0-373-86338-9

PLEASURE UNDER THE SUN

Copyright © 2014 by Lindsay Evans

For questions and comments about the quality of this book please contact us
at CustomerService@Harlequin.com.

HARLEQUIN®

Printed in U.S.A.

™ www.Harlequin.com

Dear Reader,

What condition would your heart be in if you had a harrowing experience and your young life was a roller-coaster of thrilling adventures you never wanted?

My heroine, Bailey Hughes, is still shell-shocked from childhood trauma and adult romantic misfortunes. She's far from ready for the gorgeous sculptor with the bedroom eyes eager to sweep her into his arms for nights of intense passion. Join her for this romantic journey into the unknown. I hope you'll enjoy it.

Lindsay Evans

Many thanks to Kimberly Kaye Terry
for her invaluable help on this journey of mine.
Also to Khaulah Naima Nuruddin, Sheree L. Greer,
Angela Gabriel, Brook Blander, and Keturah Israel—my
friends and supporters. The butterflies in my garden.

Chapter 1

"You are the hottest thing I've seen all night," the woman said.

She looked up to the docked yacht where Seven Carmichael stood, and watched him with a sly smile. She sipped from a glass of Scotch as she stood in the midst of the chaotic swirl of bodies on the back lawn of Marcus Stanfield's Star Island mansion. High heels. Tight jeans. A sheer white blouse showing off a lacy black bra underneath. She was a gorgeous flash in the night, something Seven could definitely appreciate, although he usually preferred his women a little less obvious. Actually, she wasn't just gorgeous. She was absolutely stunning.

His lips twitched in response to her compliment while another body part responded in a similar fashion to her sleek and sensuous body. "Thank you," he said. "You're not so bad yourself."

He'd forgotten how delightfully forward American women could be. He braced his arms against the boat's railing, watching the woman, who continued to boldly stare, hip cocked to one side, elbow of one arm resting in her palm, the crystal tumbler of Scotch held near her lips. Her gaze devoured his six-and-a-half-foot, muscled, toffee-colored frame.

"Don't worry, honey. I'm just taking in the view. I have

no intension of touching the merchandise," the woman said. "At least not yet." She smiled again, a suggestive movement of her glistening maroon lips.

"Are you so sure you could handle me?" Seven teased.

She looked him over again, brown eyes sparkling, hair swept up into an elegant pompadour. "I could handle two of you, honey."

Seven was absolutely tempted to challenge the woman on her boast. The longer he looked down at her statuesque form, with its bold swath of hair and the white silk blouse fluttering in the breeze over her lace-cupped breasts, the more his intrigue and interest grew. But… "Maybe I'll give you the chance to prove it another time," he said. "I have a twin."

The woman laughed, a husky gurgle of sound, and lifted her glass to him in salute. Then she turned on her high heels, treating him to a glimpse of her small but shapely behind in the tight jeans, and strutted down the walkway of the back lawn toward the mansion, where another party was going strong. Seven watched her go with regret, fighting the unfamiliar urge to rush after her and find out more about that heavily implied stamina of hers. He'd never been one for casual hookups, but something about that woman made him want to change his mind.

Seven stood on the deck of the yacht for a moment longer, feeling the minute movements of the *Dirty Diana* as she swayed in the dock, as much from the gentle undulations of Biscayne Bay as from the activities of the over two dozen partiers on board.

Beautiful women pranced around on the deck in their high heels. Well-dressed men—most with cigars in hand—stalked after them. Everyone was drinking and partying hard to Drake pounding from the speakers, their laughter high and bright. The hors d'oeuvres were plentiful and provided by uniformed waiters making regular trips between the mansion and boat. And at the center of it all stood Marcus Stanfield, Seven's host and recent acquaintance.

The billionaire playboy's generosity had come as a surprise to Seven, but he knew well enough from experience the whims and whimsies of the rich. He wouldn't let himself get too used to Marcus's hospitality. As quickly as it had been given, it could be taken away.

But at least Marcus's spur-of-the-moment generosity had brought Seven from the arid deserts of Dubai to a much more appealing climate. When Marcus had come to Seven's last solo show in the Arabian city, he had taken a liking to Seven's work, immediately buying two pieces and arranging to have them shipped to Miami. His attention brought Seven to the notice of a few others at the opening, including a B-list British actress whose pants Marcus was trying to get into.

The actress later hosted a dinner party for Seven at her home, where he and Marcus ended up talking for most of the night. Toward the end of the party, Marcus declared that he hadn't met anyone as interesting as Seven in a long time, and invited the artist to come with him to Miami as his guest. Seven, who had already planned on leaving Dubai, readily accepted the invitation.

Miami was his kind of town. Although he was visiting for only a short while, he could see himself settling down in a place like this. And not just for the abundance of beautiful women. It was the water, the international flavor of the city, the way certain sections reminded him of Jamaica— of Kingston, where his parents had moved from when he was a child. He was tired of living out of a suitcase, going wherever his work took him.

In the circle of hangers-on and admirers, Marcus caught Seven's eye and grinned, pointing with his glass of champagne to the two girls hanging off his arms. *Do you want some of this?* his look asked. Seven shook his head and smiled.

"No, thanks, man. Enjoy it."

The Dubai trip had worn him out. He'd spent almost two years there, finishing up the steel sculpture commissioned by the Bank of Arab Emirates. It was a prestigious commission. A well-paying one. If he wanted to, he could stop working for another two years and still live in the style to which he'd grown accustomed. But Seven liked working too much. Not to mention it was good to keep working while people still knew his name and were willing to pay exorbitant sums of money for something that came from his sweat and two hands.

In many ways, his career had been pure luck. He was lucky to have this life of his. Lucky Seven, as his mother called him. Her seventh child, the firstborn of the twins, her only children to survive past birth.

As Seven watched, one of the women from the pack surrounding Marcus separated herself and came toward him. She was short, but her stilettos gave her the much-needed height, helping to make her seem more grown-up than she actually was. Her rounded cheeks and the acne-dotted skin Seven could still see under her heavy makeup gave away her age. He would eat his welding helmet if she was even twenty-one. At thirty-five, he was far too old to be playing with children.

"What you doing out here by yourself, handsome?"

The girl tottered close, the hem of her cream-colored dress fluttering around her thighs, threatening to expose her backside. Seven vaguely remembered her from a few hours ago, when Marcus had made the introductions on the yacht. This one was filthy rich, an admitted art groupie who'd slipped her number in Seven's pocket once the introductions had been made.

She was pretty and bold, but instead of taking her to his bed, Seven wanted to clean the makeup off her face and return her to her parents.

"I'm checking out the view," Seven said with a smile.

The girl came even closer, sipping her nearly empty glass of champagne. She touched his arm, then playfully squeezed his biceps. "Yeah, me, too. And the view from where I stand is really hot." Her breath smelled like champagne and strawberries as she leaned against the railing toward him.

After the woman in the backyard, this girl seemed too self-conscious, a flashy beauty without the confidence to back it up. Seven gave the girl his most charming smile and touched her arm, saying without a word she was beautiful, but tonight wasn't the night. Her smile faltered. She clutched at the glass of champagne like a lifeline. A girl like this wasn't used to being refused anything.

"A gorgeous woman like you deserves better company than me," he said. "My head is in a whole different place tonight." He squeezed her waist and, before she could say anything else, left her in search of solitude.

Seven felt her bemused eyes on his back as he walked away, but did not turn around. As he gripped the railing to get off the yacht, Marcus swam out of his crowd of admirers to Seven's side.

"You having a good time, man?"

"You know I am." Seven slapped his host on the back.

"Good. I don't want you to get too bored." Marcus grinned as if that was an impossibility. He shoved a full glass of Scotch into Seven's hand. "Here. To make the party even better."

"If things get slow for me here, I can always head back down to the house. The action down there looks hot."

Hip-hop blared from the outdoor speakers on the back lawn of the mansion, while barely dressed women leaned from the balconies or danced suggestively to the music. Some had jumped into the pool in their party clothes, while others had simply stripped, inviting anyone else to join them with come-hither looks over their wet shoulders.

"Good, good. And don't forget you can stay here as long as you like. My place is your place. And everything in it." He inclined his head to encompass the women he'd just been talking to, one of whom was staring at him with a flirtatious come-get-it grin. She blew Marcus a kiss and he laughed, pretending to catch it and put it on his crotch.

"Thanks. I won't be staying too long at your place, though," Seven said, making a sudden decision. "I'll get my own soon. But before I get too settled here, I need to take care of a few financial things."

Most of his money was at a bank in England. He needed to set up accounts in the U.S. and arrange for his last check from the Bank of Arab Emirates to be sent there.

"That's the last thing you should worry about. I know a money guy who can help you with whatever you need."

A money guy, huh? Seven thought briefly about refusing Marcus's help. Although Seven's finances were very much in the black, in just a few short days of knowing the American billionaire, he'd received commissions worth almost three times what the bank in Dubai had paid him for the piece in their lobby. A man who made that happen probably knew a thing or two about multiplying and sheltering a fortune.

"Okay," he said. "I'll meet with your guy."

"Cool."

"Marcus, baby!" The sloe-eyed woman from across

the room had apparently gotten tired of sending her kisses long-distance. She grabbed Marcus's arm. "It's time for you to tuck me in." She grinned, all tiny teeth and bountiful cleavage.

Seven held up his hands. "Go ahead. I won't keep you from your duties."

Marcus tossed a grin his way before walking off with the woman toward the sleeping quarters belowdecks. Seven stayed only long enough to finish his Scotch. That last drink forced him to acknowledge the tiredness tugging at his shoulders and making his lids flag over his eyes. The past few days of nonstop partying with Marcus were catching up to him. Seven placed his empty glass on the tray of a passing waiter and left the boat, heading down a stone-paved path to the small cottage at the back of Marcus's mansion. Music throbbed faintly behind him, followed him on his escape from the mad party, the sounds of laughter, a body splashing into the pool.

Seven let himself into the relative comfort of the cottage, undressed and fell into the bed. It enfolded him like a lover, soft as dreams yet firm under his back. Soon, he drifted into sleep, the worries and annoyances of his third day in Miami fading away with the sounds of the music from the larger house.

"Hey, wake up, rock star!" Someone pounded at the cottage door and called out again, "Wake up!"

Seven jolted from his sleep, reaching automatically for his cell phone on the bedside table to check the time. He swore under his breath. It was just past noon. Monday. But his body felt as if it could still do with another five hours of sleep. With a groan, he scrubbed a hand over his face. In the large mirror across from the bed, his reflection gazed tiredly back at him, bleary-eyed and naked. His body, hardened from years of lifting and shaping his steel sculptures, looked almost too heavy for him to haul out of the bed.

Whoever it was knocked on the door again, forcing Seven to gather the top sheet around his bare hips and stumble to open the door. Marcus stood there, grinning.

"About time you got your lazy ass up," he said.

A trio of young women stood behind him, staring over his shoulder at Seven's bare chest and stomach. Seven was suddenly glad that he'd taken the time to cover himself, otherwise the girls would have gotten more than they'd bargained for. But, looking at the scantily dressed girls who watched him with a shark's intensity, maybe they wouldn't mind seeing him naked, after all.

"Damn," one of the girls said under her breath.

Seven cleared his throat. "Morning. It's a little early, isn't it?"

"It's never too early." Marcus laughed as if he'd made some big joke.

Behind him, the girls tittered on cue.

"You remember the girls from last night, right?" Marcus gestured to the women around him by way of introduction. Kenya was the bleached-blonde with deep gold skin. Felice wore her hair in a short natural, a pretty complement to her deep chocolate complexion. And Masiel had a fountain of black hair spilling around her narrow, foxlike face. All three girls were fiercely made up, dressed as though they'd just come from the set of a rap video.

Confused, Seven looked at the foursome gathered on his borrowed doorstep and gave them a questioning look.

"I came to take you to that money guy I told you about," Marcus said. "The girls and I are on the way to that side of town and thought you might want to tag along."

Seven raised an eyebrow at "the girls," who wore tight skirts and body-hugging blouses of the animal-print variety. They didn't look ready to see anyone's money guy. Unless he was a pimp.

Marcus read his look accurately enough. "They're not seeing the banker, you are. Come on. Get dressed. Maybe after you're done we can go grab the jet and go for a bite and a sail in Cape Cod."

Seven hesitated. He was flattered by Marcus's interest, but he had had enough of the man's hearty company. Marcus was generous, but he seemed to expect to be entertained at all times. His investment in Seven made him think the artist was there for his entertainment. It was time to end this.

"I have to shower. I don't like leaving the house dirty," Seven said.

"We'll wait."

And they did. As he walked out of the room to go shower, Marcus and the three girls sauntered into the small living area. Marcus fell into a sprawl on the couch while his companions grabbed the video game controllers and knelt in front of the fifty-inch flat screen to start a game.

In the bedroom, Seven quickly discarded the sheet and grabbed some clothes from his suitcase, climbed into the travertine-tiled shower and turned the water on full blast. The hot water washed away the last of his tiredness, flooding over his head and face, dripping through his lashes, over his mouth and down the muscular planes of his chest, belly, the thick stalk of his sex and his corded thighs. He sighed into the water, the heaviness in his body falling away to leave him awake.

Energized, he quickly finished his shower and dressed in jeans, a plain white Armani T-shirt and a favorite pair of loafers. He walked into the living room, fastening the clasp on his watch.

There, the three girls played "Just Dance," their breasts

and hips shaking as Marcus looked on with laughter and appreciation.

"Ready," Seven said.

"Yummy," Masiel murmured, turning her attention from the video game. Bouncy black waves tumbled down her back as she twisted around to look at Seven.

"I liked him better without clothes," Felice said. With her close-cropped hair and sensual mouth, she was pretty in a Meagan Good kind of way, although not as sexy.

"I'll take you however I can get you." Kenya gave up any pretense of paying attention to the game and strutted over to Seven, who stepped back before she could touch him.

He wasn't into playing with another man's toys. Marcus watched all the action with a faint smile but didn't say a word.

Seven raised an eyebrow. "You ladies are making me blush." Though clearly he was in no danger of doing that. He looked at Marcus. "Are we heading out or what?"

"Of course." Marcus stood up with a set of keys in his hand. "Let's go."

In the detached garage that was as big as another house, he chose a black Mercedes C-Class sedan and ushered the girls into the backseat before getting behind the wheel. He looked at Seven briefly. "You want to drive?"

Seven got in the passenger seat. "Yeah, right. I'm just here to relax and go along for the ride. Drive on."

Marcus chuckled.

They drove out of the garage, under the wide, slowly lifting door, into the bright spotlight of a Miami Monday afternoon. Diamond sunlight bounced off the reflective lenses of Seven's sunglasses as they wove through the estate's main drive, flanked by bright ginger plants, yellow hibiscus and a profusion of thick-stalked pink and red flamingo lilies, plants Seven was used to seeing in Jamaica.

A neatly manicured dozen or so acres, the landscape was occasionally broken by a hatted gardener stooped over a bed of flowers or stretch of grass. The smell of fresh-cut grass drifted into the car despite the closed windows and arctic AC.

The chill of the car made Seven suddenly wish for a cup of a hot chocolate. Steaming from the stove, not a packet. Freshly shaved from a ball of cocoa, swirled with milk and a dash of nutmeg. Just like his father made for him whenever he was home in Jamaica. Yeah, that was what he wanted.

Seven emerged from his momentary fantasy of hot chocolate to the sound of the girls giggling in the backseat. Marcus navigated the car through the mansion's wide double gates and out to the long bridge heading off Star Island and to the A1A for downtown.

"The firm is downtown," he said to Seven. "I'm not sure if Bailey can do anything for you today, but I let her know you'll be there soon."

"Her?"

"Yeah. Bailey. She's my money guy."

Masiel tapped Marcus's shoulder from the backseat. "Can we go shopping on Collins Avenue?"

Marcus glanced back at her in the rearview mirror. "What, you got Collins Avenue money, girl?"

A chorus of giggles sounded from behind Seven.

"Honey, we thought you'd treat us." Felice pouted, cocking a thigh bared in her short skirt. "We're always treating you," she said.

Seven didn't have to imagine what the girls were always treating Marcus to. In the rearview mirror, Masiel gave him a teasing, wet-lipped smile as she trailed a red fingernail along her low neckline. He wasn't impressed.

"You can drop me off at your money guy's office and take off," Seven said. "I got this."

"See, he got this," blond-haired Kenya mocked as she offered her cleavage for Marcus's consideration. "We have needs, Daddy." Her declaration set off another peal of laughter from the other girls.

In his profession, the rich and bored often clung to artists as a way to relieve their boredom—a lot like Marcus was doing now. Seven had seen enough of this type of leeching to last a lifetime. These girls bartered their bodies and their time for jewels or money or trips outside their small towns, riding that tiger as long as their looks lasted while hoping for one of these men to sweep them off their feet and offer marriage. He glanced at the trio in the backseat. He didn't see Marcus marrying any of them, but then again, he had underestimated women enough to know he could be wrong.

"Here it is."

The car pulled up in front of a high-rise glittering with blue glass and steel. "You're going to the top floor. Braithwaite and Fernandez Wealth Management. Ask for Bailey Hughes."

Seven nodded his thanks, patted his back pocket to make sure he had his wallet and got out of the car. As he slammed the door shut, one of the girls clambered over the other two to claim a position in the front seat beside Marcus. The younger man saluted Seven with a tap of fingers against his brow and peeled off down the street.

Inside the building, the AC threatened to turn him into an icicle in his thin white shirt and jeans. He pressed the elevator for the twenty-second floor, and when the car arrived laden with a half dozen business types who gave him cool, dismissive gazes, he got on and rose in swift quiet toward the building's summit.

* * *

The top floor was rarefied air indeed. Seven stepped off the elevator into the marble-paved lobby of Braithwaite and Fernandez Wealth Management and the cold smell of new money. A thick mahogany desk sat directly in front of the elevator. Behind the desk, a freckled redhead with wheat-colored skin watched as he walked through the steel doors of the elevator. The heels of his loafers rang out against the marble.

Seven shivered slightly in the chilled air, feeling goose bumps rise over his arms. The lobby was cold and massive. It stretched out in both directions with an impressive view of the Miami skyline to the left and an ocean of cream marble in a long corridor that branched off into several hidden hallways. Purple orchids stood in tall black planters at each corner of the large lobby, a complement to the long row of black leather armchairs lining the back wall on both sides of the elevator.

"Good afternoon," the redhead greeted him with a surprising island accent. Bahamian, if he wasn't mistaken.

"Good afternoon. I'm here to see Bailey Hughes. I was referred by Marcus Stanfield."

"Of course. Have a seat." She gestured to the thick armchairs as she lifted the phone to her ear. "Your walk-in is here," she said into the receiver. After a moment, the woman nodded. "Of course," she said then hung up the phone.

"Ms. Hughes will be with you in a moment. Would you like a beverage while you wait?"

Seven looked around the reception area at the miles of marble, at the original Rothko on the cream walls. A place of obvious wealth and influence. They'd have what he wanted. "A cup of hot chocolate if you have it," he said.

"Of course," the young woman said. She moved from

behind her desk with a click of her impressively high heels against the marble and disappeared down the hallway.

Seven shoved his hands in his pockets and strolled to the wide windows. Miami lay spread out before him, bright and glittering with its ribbons of roads, high-rise buildings and the gilded waters of Biscayne Bay. It was no Jamaica, but he looked forward to making a home here.

The sound of shoes on the marble drew his attention from the view. Two men, both middle-aged, with gray hair at their temples, one Latin and the other white, emerged from a long hallway, talking quietly. They looked up at him as they passed, nodding in quiet acknowledgment, although the white one, taller and in a more expensive suit, gave a narrow-eyed glance at Seven's jeans and T-shirt. Seven, used to the contempt of corporate types, at least until they realized how much money he made, let the man's cool-eyed stare roll off his back like bathwater.

He returned his attention to the view outside the window.

"Here you are." The pale islander returned, holding a steaming mug in both hands. She smiled, then gestured toward the long hallway the men had come from. Seven gazed longingly at the cup in her hands. "Ms. Hughes will see you now. Follow me."

She went ahead of him, long legs beautiful and eye-catching under the black skirt. At the third frosted-glass door, she stopped and knocked briefly.

"Come." A voice came faintly from behind the slightly open door.

The young woman opened the door for him and waved him inside, simultaneously handing him the hot cocoa and gesturing toward one of the leather seats in front of the desk. Her duty fulfilled, she left.

Only a brief view of the office registered: ceiling-high windows, a wide glass desk, a figure rising from behind the desk with a hand outstretched. The woman behind the desk wore gray slacks and a white blouse with a heavy white bow at her throat. Her hair, straightened and parted down the middle, was tucked behind her ears. The usual banker type. Boring and barely attractive. But *something* about her pricked Seven's memory.

"I'm Bailey Hughes. It's a pleasure to meet you," the woman said.

Seven's hand rose automatically to meet hers even as his mind registered the familiar lines of her face, her sharp blade of a body, which had drawn his attention before.

"Have we met?" he asked, shaking her hand.

Her mouthed twisted briefly in a smile. "No, we haven't. At least not formally." She drew her hand back. "And I still don't know your name." She looked up at him, challenge in the arch of her eyebrow.

He grinned. "Seven Carmichael."

"As I said before, a pleasure."

"Likewise," Seven said.

He watched her carefully, the gazellelike grace of her body, the challenging toss of her head, the long neck. Suddenly, he remembered the sound of laughter around her, the splash of bodies hitting the water. Marcus's party. Last night. The woman who had taunted him from the back lawn.

"Damn. It's you."

She laughed softly, dismissively, and drew back even more to stalk away from him—secretive smile, long legs, a fake banker's demeanor—to sit once more on the other side of her desk. In that moment, he saw that it was a mask she wore, something she pulled down to hide the vicious beauty he'd seen last night. And he was intrigued.

"Marcus told me you need help with asset management,"

she said with a cool smile. "What is it that I can do for you, Mr. Carmichael?"

He sat in the leather armchair across from her desk, with the warmth of the hot chocolate sinking into his palms, the drink nearly forgotten as he focused on something he wanted more. Seven grinned.

Chapter 2

Standing in her office was the most beautiful man Bailey had ever seen. Brown skin. A sinner's mouth. A muscled body under a loose white T-shirt and designer jeans. From the top of his sharply barbered head to the tips of the square-toed leather shoes peeking out from under his jeans, he was absolutely perfect.

Bailey gripped his hand firmly and bit her cheek at the tingle that ran through her arm, the jolt of attraction.

"Have we met?" he asked. His voice was deep, rough, with a hint of an accent. He smiled then and his teeth were like a bright light against his deep golden skin.

Bailey said something in reply but she didn't know what. This man was magnetic. She stepped away from him and put the shield of her desk between them, sinking into her chair with relief. What was wrong with her? She'd seen other attractive men before.

He arranged his lean length in the chair directly across from her and sipped the hot chocolate the receptionist, Celeste, had given him before she left. He stretched out his long legs before him, his gaze attentive, a smile crinkling the corners of his eyes. Damn, he was fine!

"Marcus told me you need help with asset management." Bailey leaned forward on her desk, hands clasped. "What is it that I can do for you, Mr. Carmichael?"

Despite his attentive gaze, Seven Carmichael looked as if he wanted to talk about anything but the reason he was in her office. He took a leisurely sip from his mug, still watching her. Bailey remembered him, too. How could she forget?

Last night at Marcus's party, she had been bored out of her mind, regretting her hasty decision to leave home for the questionable pleasures of whatever Marcus had to offer. But at home, she had felt pent up, confined by her relentless pursuit for partnership at the firm. Despite it being a weekend, she'd worked twelve hours that day alone. After only an hour at the party, she'd walked out to the dock of the mansion to get a glimpse of the bay and calm her mind before heading back to the soothing solitude of her Miami Beach condo.

The man on the deck of Marcus's pretentious little boat had appeared overhead like a dream to the soundtrack of Janelle Monáe's "Tightrope." She'd never been one for wild behavior, but frustration at having to present herself as perfectly square partnership material and as a relentless worker bee had caused another side of her emerge in that moment. So Bailey had called out to him, flirted with him in a way that she wouldn't normally have, especially if she'd known she was going to see him again.

"I want to reallocate some funds and set up local accounts," Seven said. "But that's not very important now." He chuckled, white teeth flashing against his toffee skin. "It's a small world, isn't it?"

"Yes, very. Especially when you run in Marcus's circles," she said.

Her friendship with Marcus was good for business but hell on her personal life. He'd referred enough big-money clients her way that she'd be a fool to alienate him. At the same time, all the men she'd met through him, at least the ones she'd found attractive, turned out to be assholes, criminals or both. She clenched her teeth to keep the smile on her face.

"I just met him a couple of weeks ago." Seven sat back in the chair and sipped from the black mug with the firm's monogram on it, his amused and interested gaze devouring her from the small distance. "But I didn't come here to talk about him."

On the boat he had seemed distant, not just physically but emotionally, an unattainable dream safe to flirt with. But up close here in her office, he was all personal contact and heat. A danger. Especially since he was one of Marcus's friends. Those guys, if they had money, were usually arrogant pigs who assumed their money could get them everything and everyone they wanted. If they were broke, they were parasitic hangers-on trying to jump from one well-fed fish to another. Her sister always said that was most men in Miami. Only Clive had been the exception. He had fit all her criteria but turned out to have fidelity issues.

"So what did you come in here to talk about, Mr. Carmichael?"

Seven chuckled again, another stomach-warming sound that made her want to sink deeper into her chair and hear it some more. "Call me Seven, please." That smile of his played havoc with her senses. "I came in here to talk about my money, but suddenly that idea doesn't sound as appealing, or urgent, as it did before." He glanced around her office. "Are you free for dinner tonight? I'd love to take you out and get to know you in a more intimate setting."

Yes. She wanted to say yes. But the reasons not to have dinner with him crowded in on her, forced other words past her lips.

"I've already eaten and I'll be here all evening," she said.

"I see." His lips curved in a slow, sexy smile. He sipped again from the mug of hot chocolate, licking his mouth.

"So, for the reason you're here...." Bailey prodded.

He nodded, gave another of his secret smiles and got down to business. As he spoke, Bailey sighed quietly with relief and took up her pen and pad to take notes. Seven finished his hot chocolate as they talked about his money, what he wanted to do with it, the possibility of him relocating to Miami and taking advantage of all the amenities Florida had to offer.

They didn't talk again about anything personal, certainly not about how she'd like to see him again if only he wasn't one of Marcus's friends. At the end of their hour-long conversation, he signed the papers to make their financial relationship official, shaking her hand as he stood up to leave. She took his empty mug from him and gave him a cool nod.

"Have a good evening, Mr. Carmichael."

"My name is Seven." His hand was warm around hers, firm and solid, as Bailey briefly allowed herself to imagine his body would be. Thoughts were harmless. It was no big deal to picture this beautiful man without his shirt, imagining she would get the chance to prove she could handle him as she'd boasted the previous night while the wind and his presence blew her boredom away.

"Seven." She said his name firmly.

He smiled with quiet satisfaction and turned for the door. Bailey couldn't stop herself from watching his strut across the plush carpet, the dip in his stride, the subtle press of his butt against the loosely draped jeans.

"Thank you for your business," she said, forcing her eyes up to his face. "Good luck with your relocation in Miami."

"Thank you, Bailey." Her name was a tease on his mouth.

He walked out of her office, leaving the door slightly ajar. She moved to close it but paused with the door handle in her fist, head low as she listened to his slow footsteps down the hall toward the lobby and Celeste's desk. Despite his heavy, potent masculinity, his stride across the marble floors was like a dancer's, light and graceful. Unhurried. She wondered if the way he walked was the same way he made love. Bailey shook herself, swallowing thickly. No use in dwelling on that. She closed the door and tried to put him out of her mind.

The phone abruptly rang, jolting Bailey's attention from her computer screen. She looked at her watch. It was 7:18. Celeste was long gone and, Bailey guessed, so were the partners and her assistant. Bailey looked at the number ringing through on the desk. It was an unfamiliar one.

She picked up the phone. "Yes?"

"What happened to your lovely island receptionist? She doesn't keep the same hours you do?"

Bailey took off her glasses, annoyed at herself for the leap in her belly at the sound of the Seven Carmichael's voice. "No one keeps the same hours as I do," she said dryly. "What can I do for you?"

"Well, you can start by having dinner with me."

Persistent, aren't you? A fraction of a smile touched her mouth. "I told you, I'm working for the rest of the night then I'm going home to my bed." Under her, the chair squeaked faintly as she leaned back away from her desk, turning to look out the window.

Night had settled around the building, flaring diamonds of light from the high-rises below and on the bridge marching over Biscayne Bay. Miami glittered with its particular beauty, tacky and gorgeous at the same time.

"There's a saying about Mohammed and the mountain

I won't quote to you, but you get the idea." His voice was rich with amusement, echoing oddly through the phone.

The faint sound of footsteps tilted her ear toward the hallway, an echo of what came through the phone earpiece. Someone knocked on her door. Then it opened, revealing Seven Carmichael.

"Will you call the police if I come in?"

He stood in the doorway with a picnic basket in his hand, an iPhone to his ear. He looked even better this time around with the white shirt wilted around his body from the spring heat, draping across his muscular chest like a lover's promise. The scent of hot, spiced meat and fresh bread came to her nose from his basket.

"I promise this isn't anything more sinister than dinner." He took the phone away from his ear and gave her a thoroughly unapologetic grin.

In that moment, Bailey was aware that her mouth was hanging open. She closed it with a snap. "What if I tell you I'm not hungry?" she asked, briefly turning away to save the spreadsheet on the computer before giving the man her full attention.

Against her will, she found herself examining him again, eating him up with her eyes, searching for a flaw in him. She found none.

"I don't go out with my clients," she said.

"Then I'd rather you tear up the agreement we signed earlier," he said. "Because I really, really want to go out with you."

On his tongue, the words *go out* sounded like something else altogether. Something wicked. Something delicious.

Bailey clenched her thighs together under the desk, surreptitiously licking her lips. "Stalking is illegal in this country, I hope you know," she said, tilting her head to look up at him.

"Is that what you think I'm doing?"

"Isn't it?"

He shook his head. "I'm simply bringing a beautiful woman dinner." He stepped fully into her office and pulled a folded blanket from the top of the basket. "If you want me to leave, I will. You'll miss me, though."

Seven set the basket on the floor and unpacked a feast. A roasted chicken. A salad of mixed field greens covered in red apple slices and crumbles of blue cheese. Two croissants. A bottle of chilled white wine. Bailey felt the spurt of appetite in her mouth, a flood of hunger under her palate as the smells pushed deeper in the room, tempting her.

She never ate in her office. Ever. She thought if she brought any hot food into her office, the smell would permeate the walls, the carpet, would linger and become stale and nauseating, marking her as common to the partners. Not worthy of her own corner office and the coveted partnership.

But it wasn't every day that a man brought her something without wanting anything in return.

"I don't—" *Eat in here,* she was going to say. But watching him kneel on the blanket, the thin white material of his T-shirt stretching over the muscles of his back as he made their dinner, the words curled up in her mouth then slid back down her throat. "I don't have any dishes," she said instead.

"All taken care of." He jerked his head toward a place beside him on the blanket. "Come sit and have something to eat. The sooner you eat your dinner, the sooner you can throw me out." He flashed her a smile that swayed her resolve even more.

Bailey kicked off her shoes and sat on the blanket. Even with the competing aroma of the food, she could detect his scent, a woodsy cologne, the faint tang of sweat. He smelled of masculinity and the outdoors.

"I didn't invite you in here to bring me dinner." She tried to make her words firm but knew they were as melting as butter left out in the sunlight. Bailey took a slice of apple and felt its satisfying, juicy crunch between her teeth.

"I know. You didn't invite me in here at all, but I appreciate you opening your door." Seven brought out two plastic plates, forks and clear cups.

"I'm sure you know what I'm going to say next."

"Yes, I do. But save all that love talk for later."

Bailey shook her head, reluctantly smiling. Seven pulled a small stack of napkins from the basket and put it in the ocean of space Bailey had left between them. "I got all this from Whole Foods, so I assume it's all organic and good for you, in case that's a concern." Seven tugged a chicken leg free and began to eat. "Go ahead," he said, chewing.

Bailey tucked her feet under her on the blanket, glanced up at him through her lashes, at his smiling mouth glistening from the chicken juices.

"Okay."

She made a small sandwich from a croissant, chicken and bits of the salad. The food was good. Her croissant was buttery and warm around the perfectly seasoned pieces of chicken, faintly bitter greens, sweet apples and crumbly blue cheese. Beside her, Seven ate with rich appetite, quickly finishing the chicken leg before reaching into the golden-brown bird to rip out a piece of the breast with his long fingers. Her stomach fluttered.

"I appreciate you making time in your evening to see me," Seven said after finishing his latest mouthful.

"You didn't give me much of a choice."

"Yes, I did. You know that better than anyone."

He was right. She could have called the police. Called security. Or even pointed to the door and demanded he leave immediately. He didn't seem the type to ignore a woman's wishes. But that was an assumption based on absolutely nothing. The last time she'd assumed so much, she'd ended up with a tarnished engagement ring and a lifetime of embarrassment.

Seven ripped a croissant in two, watching her carefully. "If you want me to leave, I will. You never have to worry about me forcing myself on you. Never."

She shook her head. "It's not that. I—"

A knock interrupted her. "Ms. Hughes, are you still here?"

She froze with a piece of chicken in her mouth. One of the firm's partners was at the door. A brief flutter of panic rippled through her stomach. She thought they'd all gone home. Quickly, she finished chewing, wiped her hands on a napkin and stood up to open the door. Her boss Harry Braithwaite stood on the other side, briefcase in hand.

"Good evening, Mr. Braithwaite." She smiled at her boss, blocking the view into the office with her body. "Yes, I'm still here. Taking care of a few last-minute details with the Wallace-Chatham account." That wasn't a complete lie. She'd been poring over the paperwork when Seven called.

Bailey fought the urge to curl her bare toes self-consciously in the carpet, hoping he hadn't seen them. Going barefoot in the office was heavily frowned upon, especially by the raving germaphobe Raphael Fernandez. But bare feet made her feel unfettered and free, especially in the glass prison her office could at times become.

"That is a tricky one, isn't it?" Harry said. His nose twitched.

Did he smell the food in her office? Would he ask to come in and talk about the account?

Bailey cleared her throat. "Nothing I can't handle."

He nodded briskly. "Good. That's just the kind of attitude we like for a partner to have." Mr. Braithwaite nodded again, eyes flickering behind her to look into her office. "Keep up the good work. I'll see you in the morning."

Bailey released a quiet breath. "Have a good night, Mr. Braithwaite."

He thanked her and headed down the hallway for the elevators. He and Raphael had been dangling the partnership carrot in front of her for the past few months now, stressing how a Braithwaite and Fernandez partner should act, react and behave. And Bailey was success-driven enough to leap for that carrot. With a broken engagement now two years behind her and no immediate prospects for a family of her own, this was something she wanted more than ever.

Her sister, Bette, thought she was being downright ridiculous about the partnership thing. But her sister never worried about anything. For her, life was one big expensive party where someone else always picked up the tab. She was as carefree about life as Marcus. Only he could actually afford to be. Bette could not.

Bailey waited until Mr. Braithwaite was halfway down the hallway before she went back into her office.

Seven's eyebrow quirked with mischief. "Did I almost get you in trouble?"

"Hardly," she said. "This is not the principal's office."

"Not unless you're the sexy teacher, and in that case, I'll be more than happy to be your naughty student." He grinned.

She shook her head. "No."

But his teasing was infectious. She almost smiled as she sat back on the blanket next to him and picked up the remains of her sandwich. Her boss hadn't noticed anything. And if he had, he hadn't said a word about it. Surely, something like this couldn't affect her chances of getting the partnership. She dismissed Harry Braithwaite from her mind and bit into the sandwich.

"You need to relax," he said. "It's a job. Not your life."

"For me, it's the same thing." She covered her mouth with one hand as she answered him, still chewing.

"Then we need to change that."

We?

Bailey laughed. Seven's audacity and the way he stirred her sleeping libido made her want to prolong these moments in his company. He was charming, almost unnaturally beautiful, and she liked him. A lot.

Seven opened the bottle of white wine and poured some into two of the plastic cups.

"I can't." Bailey held up a hand in refusal. "I'm working, remember?"

"It's just sparkling grape juice." He lifted the cup and brought it to her mouth. "Here, see for yourself."

Bailey blushed, warmed by his nearness, the low and intimate sound of his breathing. She smelled his musk, the kiss of sweat on his skin, and swayed closer. Her thoughts flickered on and off like a dying light bulb. *Don't touch him. Tell him to leave. You can't afford this kind of man in your life. God! He smells so good.*

She'd never felt this deep an attraction for someone. It frightened her a little. Made her want to draw back from the simple offering he made. Seven's dark, curly-lashed eyes peered deeply into hers, as if he was offering her more than grape juice. She opened her mouth and tasted the crisp sweetness of what he gave her. The grape juice effervesced over her tongue. An unexpected bite of spice made her mouth tingle. She sneezed.

Seven laughed. "It has ginger in it."

"Damn. Ginger always makes me sneeze." To prove it, she sneezed again.

He sipped from the same cup he'd asked her to taste. "That is adorable."

His laughter mingled with the sound of her cell phone's ring tone. Smiling, Bailey wiped her nose with a napkin and stood to grab her phone off the desk. Marcus's image and name flashed on the phone's display. For a moment, she debated not answering. The last thing she wanted to do was deal with Marcus and his foolishness, especially when she'd managed to all but forgive and forget that he was a friend to her good-looking and damn near irresistible office guest.

Bailey sighed and picked up the call. "Hi, Marcus."

Seven looked up when she mentioned his friend's name, a frown on his otherwise smooth forehead. Then he looked away, busying himself with taking something out of the picnic basket. Bailey sank down into her chair and turned her attention back to the phone call.

"You sound happy," Marcus said.

"Don't make it seem like such an unusual occurrence."

"Isn't it? You're the only chick I'd ever tell she needs to get laid. Since Clive, you act like you've been saving the kitty for marriage."

Bailey's good mood abruptly evaporated. "What do you want, Marcus?"

He had the nerve to laugh in her ear. "I was calling to check on my boy, Seven. Did you take care of him?"

"We're talking right now," she said.

Marcus whistled. "Damn. It's like that?" He laughed again, this time with a whole other meaning behind it.

"No. It's not." Bailey's face flushed with heat, but she kept her voice hard.

"This is shocking the hell out of me. You don't have time for any man that's not—"

"Get to the point, please. I have things I need to get back to."

"I bet you do." He chuckled, a low and dirty sound.

"Anyway, tell Seven that Nilda wants to buy one of his pieces. I'm with her right now. I tried to call his cell but he's not picking up."

Bailey knew Nilda. Another one of Marcus's friends with more money than sense.

"Pieces?"

"Yeah. Your new boyfriend likes to hammer on things and sell them as art. Chicks can't get enough of him or his stuff."

"He's a sculptor?"

Seven looked up at her tone of voice. Bailey turned away from him to stare, blinking, out the window. "You didn't mention that before."

"Does it matter? You want clients and he's got money to help you get that corner office." The sound of laughter and a popped bottle of champagne gurgled to Bailey through the phone. "Anyway, I gotta go. Pass my message on to the man, will you? He can call me if he wants to get together later." Marcus hung up.

Slowly, Bailey did the same. An artist.

It made sense. All along, there had been something about Seven that reminded Bailey of her father—her dear broke and irresponsible father.

"You didn't tell me you were an artist," she said, voice brittle with the frost of her disappointment.

Frowning, Seven slowly got up from the floor and sat in the chair across from her desk, putting them at a relatively even height. "You look upset. Why does it matter?"

"It matters." Bailey clenched her fist and realized she still held the cell phone in her hand. She put it on the desk and leaned back in her chair. The fact that he was Marcus's friend, she could have possibly overlooked, but this… This slammed the door on every possibility between them.

"What's the problem?" he asked.

Suddenly, Bailey felt tired. The stress of her day and the seesaw of emotions from Seven's appearance hit her like a Mack truck.

"Actually, there's no problem," she said.

"If that isn't giving me mixed messages, I don't know what is." Seven raised an eyebrow in her direction. "What is it? You don't like artists. Did one break your heart or something?"

"I have a lot to do tonight. Can you just pack all this stuff up and go, please?" She slipped her stockinged feet into the four-inch black Manolo Blahnik pumps under her desk to regain some semblance of power in the conversation.

Seven leveled a steady gaze at her. "Okay," he said.

Although his movements seemed slow and unhurried, he quickly gathered the remains of their impromptu picnic into the basket and tucked them away. Soon, he stood at the door, ready to leave.

"Thanks for stopping by," Bailey said. Even with every disastrous thing she now knew about him, she still wanted to rush over to Seven and ask him to stay. *Beg* him to stay. "It's unfortunate we won't be working together, after all." Slowly, she stood up to her full height and then some in the couture stilettos, giving him her coolest and most professional smile.

He held her gaze for a long moment before responding. "Yes, a shame." Then he was gone.

Bailey's smile withered away. After his faint footsteps had faded down the hallway, she stood in the middle of her office, with the after-fragrance of their picnic swirling around her, disappointment like ashes on her tongue.

She left the office shortly after Seven did, unable to concentrate on work. With him gone, the building seemed lonely in a way it hadn't before. Lonely and cold. Bailey gathered her briefcase, turned off the lights in her office and got on the elevator, pressing the button for the parking garage.

The last time a man had intrigued her as much as Seven, she'd quickly opened herself to him, excited that, for the first time in her twenty-eight years, she felt something close to love, a feeling her sister always swam in like some rarified pool in an otherwise dry universe. Bailey had almost drowned. She hadn't realized that Clive, a professor at the University of Miami, had been steadily sleeping his way through his graduate students. Even after he'd asked her to marry him.

Bailey's heels clicked a sad tattoo against the cement floor of the garage. Although it was almost nine in the evening, hers wasn't the only car in the well-lit parking structure. She pressed a key on the remote and it chirped once, unlocking the pale blue Volvo C70 with a quick flash of the headlights. She climbed in and turned on her stereo and the Alice Smith song that had been playing on her way to work blasted into the small confines of the car. The bluesy, big-throated song blew away her unproductive thoughts about her love life and anything else lurking in her subconscious.

With the top down, she drove to her beachside condo, enjoying the feel of the wind in her hair during the short drive. She knew the route well and had driven it most of the eight years she'd been working at Braithwaite and Fernandez. It hadn't been her first job offer after graduating from the University of Miami with her degrees in finance and business administration, but it was the one that had the most potential for growth and allowed her to stay in Miami. Stability. She had it. And it was something she was grateful for.

In the condo, she put her keys on the silver-plated hook by the door, walking by moonlight into the living room to drop her briefcase on the couch, then detouring in the kitchen to grab a crystal tumbler from the cupboard. Ice cubes clinked against the glass as she held it under the fridge's dispenser. At the sideboard in the sitting room, she poured Scotch into the tumbler. The liquor gurgled and splashed over the ice in the silence.

Seven Carmichael briefly floated through her thoughts as she took the first sip of the twelve-year-old single malt. He had been like the drink, a searing heat through her senses that put her on pause for a moment to pay close attention to the slow burn over her tongue, in her chest and her belly.

Bailey shook him from her head.

It had been a long day, but she was far from tired. Her work energized her. And though she would have liked to share the evening with someone—the silver rush of moonlight over her hardwoods, the coolness of the floor against her bare feet, her quiet walk back out of her condo and up the elevator to the rooftop pool—she also savored her privacy. Her things.

Her home was all paid for. So was her car. She owed no one. It was a great feeling. One she cherished even as she sat at the edge of the pool with moonlight and starlight winking overhead, her whiskey by her hand. Alone.

Chapter 3

"If I'd known you were going to make a play for her, I would have warned you." Marcus braced his elbows against the bar, sipping from his Hennessy and Coke. "Unless you're corporate, you're wasting your time."

"Why? Is she just about money?" Seven asked.

He hadn't gotten that vibe from her at all, and she had seemed to warm to him over the course of the hour they'd spent together on her office floor. But that warmth had disappeared once Marcus opened his big mouth and told her what Seven did for a living.

Seven tilted the last of his beer to his lips and leaned back in the chair at the bar of Marcus's favorite spot, Gillespie's Jazz and Martini Bar. The sound of the piano wove through the lazy Monday night, while soft laughter, the clink of glasses, the flash of jewels imbued the air with a subdued urban magic.

"Nah," Marcus said dismissively. "She doesn't care about things like that. Her last man was a teacher, some professor over at UM. She just doesn't do artists."

Seven looked at him. "If you knew that, why did you tell her that?"

"Like I said, man. I didn't know you were feeling her like that. Most guys, once they realize she's such a hard-ass, they back off. She's hot, but damn!" Marcus shook his head.

Seven breathed in the memory of Bailey. Everything about her was hot. Her body. The way she had thawed for him like an ice sculpture under the rising sun. And her smile—absolutely incredible.

"Just give it up, man." Marcus raised his drink to his lips. "You're better off."

Seven made a noncommittal sound. After what had happened in Bailey's office, he'd been in a hurry to distance himself from Marcus, convinced that the other man was bad luck for his new life in America. He had left Braithwaite and Fernandez to view a condominium with vacancies. Luckily, they allowed him to move in immediately. When Marcus called to invite him to Gillespie's, Seven had reluctantly accepted, plugging the address into the GPS and making his way to the club.

"You're not going to give up, are you?" Marcus asked, his tone of voice saying that Seven should give up.

"Why should I?"

"I already gave you a good reason. Bailey is a genius with money, but she's a bitch. Plain and simple."

"Every strong woman isn't a bitch, Marcus."

"Spoken like a man who's already whipped. And she didn't even give you any."

Seven gestured to the bartender for another beer. "Spoken like a man who's never had a special woman in his life."

"I've had plenty of special women." Marcus laughed.

Seven nodded his thanks as the bartender slid him another bottle of Corona with lime.

"And speaking of which…" Marcus swiveled around in his chair as two women walked up to them, parting the crowd with their video-girl good looks. It was two of the girls from earlier that day. "Felice and Masiel are here for our pleasure," he said, pulling Felice against him. The girl settled into his chest with a satisfied purr while her friend looked at Seven expectantly.

Seven squeezed the lime into his beer then slid the crinkled remnants of the citrus into the full bottle. "I don't need any company tonight, thanks." He sipped his beer, mouth puckering at the tartness of lime and beer.

Marcus stared at him in amazement. "You're refusing this?" He gestured to Felice's lush frame while she posed seductively, hand on hip, breasts thrust out.

"You're hot like fire, baby," Seven reassured the woman. "But I'm not in the mood."

"Damn. You *are* whipped." He started to sing Babyface's "Whip Appeal" in a surprisingly good voice.

Seven laughed despite his irritation. "Forget you, man. I'm heading out. See you later." He put the beer to his head, drinking as much as he could, then thudded the mostly full bottle against the bar with a sound of finality. He stood.

"You're going to regret giving this up," Marcus said. "But that's cool. I'll handle the girls for you."

Masiel claimed the seat Seven had vacated, giving him her sexiest hurt look.

"Enjoy." Seven tipped his imaginary hat at Marcus in a mocking salute, then turned and left the bar.

He didn't have a particular destination in mind. His only goal was to get away from Marcus and his poison so he could have some time to himself. To think. To just be. But as Seven climbed into the rental Lexus and drove away from the bar, he suddenly realized that what he wanted more than anything was to go for a swim. Although he'd been in Miami for four long days, he had yet to get in the water. It had been months since he'd been in the water, not since his trip to Jamaica last winter to visit his parents.

Even then, he'd spent most of his time helping his parents around the house—fixing, climbing, painting, all good and honest work that left a pleasant ache in his body and sharpened his hunger for the good food his mother always had in the kitchen. A pang of homesickness took him, and Seven stepped harder on the gas, pushing the car up Collins Avenue toward his new condo. Once there, he quickly parked, went upstairs to change into his swim trunks and a white jogging suit, then walked the two blocks to the beach.

It was dark. The beach was deserted except for the occasional passerby. Waves tumbled up on the sand, pale waves painting the sand dark as they capered up on the beach before retreating back into the ocean. Seven kicked off his sandals and pulled off his jogging suit. The water called him.

Chapter 4

Bailey didn't realize she'd brought her phone up to the roof with her until it rang. She put down her Scotch—her third glass in the past two hours—to answer it. "Good evening, Bette."

Her sister chuckled into the phone. "Hello, sister dear. Did you finally leave the office?"

"Yes. Thank you very much."

Bette made a shocked noise. "It's not even midnight."

There had been many nights when Bette had called her as late as two in the morning to find Bailey still at the office, laboring over some account or other. Worthless things, her sister said, despite the fact that her clients were worth billions and she handled millions of dollars of their money.

"What happened to drag you out of your den?"

"Who says something happened?" But something in her tone must have warned Bette.

"Ooh," her sister gasped, drawing out the exhalation like caramel. "Do tell!"

Bailey picked up her Scotch and brought it to her lips. "There's nothing to tell."

"Shut up with your lies, girl!"

Bailey was helpless to the slight smile that quirked her lips. An image of Seven came to her, his hand raised to lift the plastic cup of sparkling white grape juice to her mouth. His own mouth smiling.

"It's nobody."

"Well, if he made you leave the office at a reasonable hour, I want to meet this nobody."

"He's..." She felt the disappointment again. "He's like our parents."

"What...dead?"

Bailey hissed. Sometimes she wondered what was wrong with her sister. "No. He's some sort of artsy type. He sculpts or something."

"Not this again." She could practically see her sister plop down on the nearest available surface, flip her long dreads over her shoulder with irritation and scowl into space. "The life we had with Mama and Daddy wasn't so bad."

"What are you *talking* about? There were months when we were damn near homeless."

"But didn't we have so much *fun?*" Bette stretched out the last word as if it was the most important part of their lives. Damn the unpaid bills and insecurity about the roof over their heads, or where their next meal was coming from, or the constant moving from place to place following one art residency or another. There were nights when Bailey had cried over the desperation of it. She hated that life. The thought of going back to something like it terrified her.

Bailey sighed and took a sip of her Scotch. It seared across her tongue in a wave of beautiful heat, flowed down her throat like liquid silk. She stood at the edge of the cordoned-off rooftop to look down on the trickle of evening traffic, the winking lights from the occasional passing car. Bette was talking, but she tuned her sister out. They could never agree on their life before Miami. It was as if they had lived different versions of the same story. For Bette, it had been a dream. For Bailey, it had brought nothing but nightmares.

A movement on the beach caught her attention. For a moment, she didn't know what it was, but the shape coalesced into a masculine silhouette walking out from the water. A dark, muscled figure with long, lean legs and slim hips covered in tight white swim trunks.

"What?" Bette's voice cracked at her through the phone.

"Huh?"

"Did you say something?" her sister asked.

Bailey cleared her throat. "No, I didn't say a thing."

"You weren't listening to me, either, were you?"

She leaned over the balcony, trying to see the man more clearly. "Not really."

"Typical." Her sister made a noise of frustration. "I don't even know—"

"There's a really hot guy on the beach."

"Really?" Bette asked, her irritation apparently forgotten. "What does he look like?"

The waves whispered like a siren in the quiet evening. On the sand, the man stood with his hands on his hips, staring into the dark water. There was something vaguely familiar about him, about the masculine perfection of his body close enough for her to see his sculpted back with its deeper shadows of muscle.

"I can't really tell, but his body is ridiculous," Bailey murmured as she leaned over the concrete barrier. It pressed into her ribs through her blouse.

She'd seen enough body-conscious gay men walking on the beach that she wasn't easily impressed. This specimen below her was something else. A brief thought of the man who'd brought dinner to her office intruded. But she shoved it away. It was easier to be frivolous and giggly with her sister, someone who wouldn't take her appreciation of a stranger's body for anything other than what it was.

"Does he look like Tyrese?" Bette asked with a laugh. "Damn, maybe it *is* Tyrese."

"No. This man looks much better." *Oh, my God, so much better.* "I wish I had my binoculars."

"Now you're just being creepy."

"No. Just appreciative."

"And drunk, too, I expect." Bette laughed, a low and happy sound that made Bailey smile. "I wish I could come over there and have some of what you're sipping on. And check out that hottie for myself."

"No one told you to move all the way to Fort Lauderdale. There's nothing up there but old queens."

"And me."

Bailey made a rude noise. "How could I forget?" She leaned her hip against the stone railing, paying proper attention to her sister while keeping her eyes on the man on the beach.

"Speaking of queens, I'm coming down to Miami to do work for a Colette fashion show this week." Bette made a flippant sound as if her being the makeup artist of choice for one of the biggest fashion names in the industry was nothing. "You should take me to dinner and invite me to spend the rest of the week with you."

Bailey smiled. "Sure. *Mi* condo *es su* condo." She purposely didn't say anything about taking her sister to dinner.

Bette noticed, of course, and muttered something about Bailey being a cheapskate, although they both knew that the dinner would happen—probably multiple times in the week—and that Bailey would pay.

Her sister was quiet for a moment, and Bailey heard only her low breathing, the rustle of some sort of plant, as though she was outside in the backyard of her rented Wilton Manors house.

"You know you have to get over this thing about men like Daddy," Bette said.

"What about you and your thing about women like Mama?"

"I'm not even going to justify that with an answer." For once, her sister sounded incredibly grown-up, coolly attempting to put Bailey in her place. "I'm not shutting a whole population of people out of my dating pool just because they don't have the kind of job you find ideal."

"I'm not going to compromise myself—"

"It's not compromise when you're making yourself miserable going after guys like Clive, who aren't worth anything. I'm sure the guy you were lusting after is great if you'll just give him a chance."

"I don't think so," Bailey muttered.

On the beach, the man turned away from the water and began to pull on his clothes. He shoved his feet in sandals and threw something—probably a shirt—over his shoulder. A sixth sense must have warned him about her watching, because he looked up. And Bailey lost her breath. She was dimly aware of him raising a hand in acknowledgment. Then, instead of waiting on a response from her, the man walked up the sand away from the water, and away from her. Bailey blinked as she watched the dark figure disappear down a narrow side street.

It was Seven Carmichael.

Chapter 5

Bailey couldn't stop thinking about him. At work the next day, he lingered in her mind like the sound of the sea, haunting and unforgettable. Long after his figure had disappeared from below her at the beach, Bailey had allowed her thoughts, loosened by the Scotch, to dwell on the most beautiful man she had seen. Bette had tried to talk her into seeing him again, but Bailey refused to listen to her. Just because he had a hot body—a damn near perfect body, in fact—didn't mean she should just throw her principles out of the window.

"That's exactly what that means," Bette had said with a happy lilt to her voice.

Wasn't Bailey the one who had been drinking?

"Aren't you supposed to be gay or something?"

"Bisexual," Bette had corrected. "I can't wait to see this guy. It's too bad we're not identical twins. I could get his cookies and he'd never know the difference."

"I think you've been sleeping with women too long. Guys don't have 'cookies,' Bette."

"Oh, yes, they do, sister dear."

Bailey had almost hung up the phone on her. After their call, she'd felt regretfully sober. She'd left the comfort of her balcony for a long shower, where her thoughts had lingered over the picture Seven made on the beach—muscled back, tight body, lean grace in every movement.

"I don't want him!" Bailey had said to her reflection in the bathroom mirror as she combed out her wet hair. No one in the room had believed her.

The next morning, she tried to focus despite an unexpected hangover. A virgin Bloody Mary and too many cups of coffee later, she still didn't feel 100 percent. In her office, she was sluggish, forcing her mind from thoughts of her comfortable bed to the task at hand.

Her client Raymond Gooden sat in her office, carefully glancing over the papers she had just presented for him to sign. Bailey took a deep breath of relief. The headache was finally going away, and at least he didn't seem to notice her sluggishness. She'd managed to present nothing but a competent, businesslike front to her client as they'd discussed plans for investing the latest three-million-dollar payoff from his European film investments.

Wearing a red tie, body-conscious suit and trendy haircut, he seemed to be taking advantage of all the perks of his money, but contrary to appearances, Mr. Gooden was very cheap. If he ever asked Bailey out, he'd probably expect her to pay.

She flicked her gaze across her desk at the fiftysomething-year-old man. Why was she thinking about this man asking her out? Just because Seven Carmichael... Bailey clamped down on her thoughts and forced herself back to the matter at hand.

"What do you think, Raymond? Are these figures to your liking?"

"These numbers are fine with me," Mr. Gooden said, offering a slight smile.

As soon as Raymond Gooden left her office, she gathered his paperwork, slipped it into his file and put it in the outbox for her secretary. Bailey had digital backups of everything, but she enjoyed the touch of paper. It gave her a sense of security the intangible digital material did not have. Funny, since people would say what she did with money—trading, multiplying and moving it around in a world far removed from paper—was the ultimate triumph of the intangible over tangible. But she didn't care; she lived with her contradictions as well as anyone else.

As she flipped through her notepad to see what notes needed transcribing, someone knocked on her door.

"Come in," she called out.

She'd expected her secretary coming in to tell her she was heading out to lunch, but instead, it was Raphael Fernandez, the less appealing of her two bosses. He came into her office, took a small bottle of antibacterial spray from his pocket, spritzed his hands, then wiped them on a handkerchief he took from his breast pocket. Apparently, he'd had to touch her germ-ridden doorknob on the way in. Raphael swept inside, attempting to take up most of the space in her office. Luckily, they'd given her enough square footage so that wasn't possible. So instead, he loomed over her desk.

In a tailored charcoal suit, with his handkerchief once again tucked into the pocket of his jacket, and an American flag lapel pin, Raphael presented the perfect picture of a wealthy and patriotic gentleman. Though he dressed the part of an urbane man about town, his face was like a fighter's—rough-looking, with a scar slashing across his right cheek and a nose that looked as though it had been broken a few times. It was a contradiction that pleased the clients. Maybe they thought he was one who would protect their money at all costs.

"Bailey," he said. Unlike Mr. Braithwaite, Raphael preferred the more casual approach. Although, with him, his use of her first name was almost patronizing. It was a skill

Bailey sometimes marveled at. "Harry told me you were here working until the small hours last night."

"Not that late, Raphael. A few things came up with a potential client. It didn't take very long. Mr. Braithwaite caught me when I looked the busiest." She gave him a cool smile.

"Nevertheless, I wanted to tell you that you're doing a good job. Your work here at the firm has not gone unnoticed."

"Thank you, Raphael. I'm merely doing my job."

"And doing it in an exceptional way," he said.

Although she didn't like Raphael as much as she did Mr. Braithwaite, she found that he had a grudging respect for her that made itself known at the most bizarre of times. Like now. She merely leaned back in her chair, lacing her fingers together under her chin to watch him posturing, instead of entering into a battle with him over the physical position of power in the room. The scar on his cheek lifted his mouth in a vaguely menacing smile.

Bailey smiled back at him.

Raphael smiled again in approval and stepped back, ready to leave her office. Then something on her desk caught his eye. Her notepad.

"Do you know Seven Carmichael?"

She looked down at her desk to see what he'd noticed. Seven's name scrawled on the yellow legal pad along with some financial figures.

"Ah, yes. He came in yesterday for a consultation. He's relocating to the Miami area and is on the hunt for a local firm to handle a few things for him."

"Did he bite?"

"No. I don't think he'd be a good fit for us."

"Good fit? My dear, this man is worth millions. Not just that, his art is being collected by every bank and bored housewife with a garden. Get him to change his mind and come with us." He lifted an eyebrow. "Unless you don't want that partnership, after all."

Bailey winced. Not this again. Every time she thought she'd done something good enough to catch the attention of the partners, another test or hurdle appeared. Would it end? Bailey clenched her back teeth, cursing herself for not ripping off the page with Seven's name and throwing it away when she first got into the office.

"Okay," she said. "I'll see what I can do."

Bailey almost slammed the door into Raphael Fernandez's back as he left her office. Was she really going to do this? She looked down at the traitorous notepad with Seven's name written in her clear cursive. She hadn't written down more than a few notes under his name, but that had been enough to bring him to her boss's notice. Bailey cursed softly.

After work, she resisted the urge to call Bette. Her sister would only laugh at her for wanting the partnership so badly. With most things in Bailey's life, her sister was able to listen, laugh and commiserate over the appropriate adult beverage, but this job at Braithwaite and Fernandez was something Bette didn't understand. She thought the job was getting much more out of Bailey than she got out of it, and if she ever got the partnership, that inequality would only get worse.

She had a sneaking suspicion that Bette was right. With that depressing thought, she pulled her car into the Whole Foods parking lot near her office to grab a few essentials for the week. She slung her purse over her shoulder and stepped from the car, pressing the remote to lock the convertible and turn on the alarm. There was a grocery list in her purse somewhere. She rifled through the thick black bag, still making her way toward the entrance of the store.

"Bailey Hughes, is that you?"

She looked up from her purse, empty-handed at the sound of the familiar voice. *Oh, great.*

For once, she'd left work at a reasonable hour, so the parking lot was full of the after-work crowd doing the same thing she was. She'd barely been able to find a parking spot. If anyone asked her later on, she'd use that as an excuse for why she didn't look in the right direction when she first heard Clive call her name. She glanced once over her shoulder, knowing he wasn't behind her, then kept walking toward the entrance of the store, moving swiftly through the crosswalk and past slow-moving pedestrians.

"Bailey!"

Damn. He was almost in front of her, walking briskly toward her at an angle from the store's exit. It was hard not to notice him there, an attractive man of medium height, light brown complexion and startling hazel eyes.

He headed directly for her from the grocery store, pushing a shopping cart with a toddler strapped into the attached child seat. A brown-skinned woman with a long ponytail walked next to him. She carried her purse over one shoulder and distractedly scrolled through something on her cell phone. He stopped the cart a few feet from Bailey, forcing her to acknowledge him.

"Clive." She greeted him with a deliberate lack of enthusiasm. "It's been a long time." *I wish it had been longer.*

"I thought that was you. I haven't seen you around in a while."

"Why? Were you looking for me?"

At her words, the woman looked up from her phone. Her eyes narrowed as she took in Bailey, from the top of her perfectly pressed and sculpted hair to the tips of her

Jimmy Choo black python ankle boots. Bailey may have felt like hell this morning when she left home, but she had been determined to look good. The woman put her phone away and sidled closer to her husband.

He chuckled. "Of course I wasn't looking for you. But I do know you don't work too far from here. Remember how you used to go crazy for the chicken wings at this place?" He jerked his head toward the market.

That's what you remember about me?

Bailey shrugged, then looked past him toward the store. How much longer was he going to prolong this?

"Oh, this is my wife. Charmaine." He gestured to the woman, who tucked her hand in the crook of his arm and smiled brightly at Bailey. A child. She barely looked twenty-five.

"Hello." Bailey greeted her with the smile she didn't have for Clive.

She didn't give the woman her name. The girl looked young enough to be one of his graduate students, which was probably what she had once been. From the way Charmaine was holding on to Clive, she was well aware of his inability to keep his penis in his pants when away from home. Charmaine stroked the toddler's curly Afro.

The child grinned and waved his arms. "Dada."

"And this is our son, Kofi." Clive touched the child's arm flailing in his direction.

"That's great," Bailey said to Charmaine. "You have a handsome boy there." She nodded toward the child in the shopping cart so the girl wouldn't mistake her meaning.

Charmaine's smile widened. "Thank you. Isn't he just? Clive and I are working on a little sister or brother for him to play with."

"How sweet," Bailey said. *Did I really need to know that?*

"So what are you doing these days?" Clive asked.

"Grocery shopping."

He gave a hearty and fake laugh. "You were always so funny, Bailey. How could I ever forget that about you?"

"Yes, how could you?"

She, Clive, Charmaine and the baby stood in uncomfortable silence for a moment. Then Bailey had enough. She nodded at the young woman. "It was good to meet you, Charmaine, but I have to run. Clive, take care of yourself."

She walked away before her ex-fiancé could say anything else. There was only so much a woman could take in one day.

Chapter 6

Seven couldn't stop thinking about Bailey Hughes. The woman occupied his waking days and dreaming nights. His body seemed in a permanent state of arousal around her, hard and ready to take hers. Palms itching to stroke her skin. Mouth ready to taste Bailey, to savor her. It was no wonder that he thought he saw her everywhere. That night after the beach, he swore he had seen her watching him from the top of a nearby building. Before he thought better of it, he'd waved, wondering only later if his mind had been playing tricks on him.

He sat at an outdoor table of a little bistro in Miami Beach, waiting on his lunch. There was food at home and within walking distance, too, but he didn't feel like cooking it. Marcus had invited him over for lunch with a couple of his "good friends"—females, no doubt—but Seven didn't feel like dealing with that, either. Settled into his new apartment, he was now on the hunt for a separate studio space in town so he could start working. His obsession with Bailey would fade to the background once he fired up the welder and immersed his body into shaping steel to his will. At least he hoped so.

"Here you go, sir." The waitress settled a plate in front of him—grilled Atlantic salmon marinated in coconut milk and spices, served on a bed of firm, dark green asparagus.

"Thank you." He leaned back in his chair while she laid a set of utensils wrapped in a white cloth napkin next to the steaming plate.

"Can I get anything else for you?" Her tone was slightly flirtatious, flattering.

The girl was pretty, dark skinned with a short and sexy Afro. In a few short words when she'd first come to get his order, she'd let him know that she was available for nearly anything once she got off work, or even for a few minutes on her break. But Seven had only smiled in thanks for the offer, leaving it firmly where it lay.

"I'm perfectly happy with this," he said. "Thank you."

She shrugged in acceptance, offered him a generous smile and left him in peace. He wouldn't be surprised to see her phone number under the plate when he was done.

Seven picked up his fork and began to eat.

The outdoor seating of the restaurant was near to the sidewalk, cordoned off from the pedestrians by a three-feet-high white railing. Seven watched the traffic as he ate, relaxed and happy to be doing nothing that involved socializing for a while. Being around Marcus often meant being in the company of at least half a dozen people he didn't know. For the most part, it wasn't a problem. But sometimes he just wanted to sit back in silent solitude and enjoy the day. It was hard doing that in a roomful of people. He breathed in the sea air and leaned back in his chair, chewing on a bite of salmon.

Just then, he noticed a woman walking down the sidewalk toward him and carrying on an animated discussion on a cell phone. Red skirts swinging, high heels dancing against the sidewalk, wearing some sort of old-fashioned square-collared white blouse. Long dreadlocks piled high on top of her head. Very striking. Seven looked at her face again. He drank from his glass of water and deliberately took in everything about the woman, from the way she moved to the way she gestured as she spoke. He stood up.

"Excuse me, miss," he called out.

She still had a few feet before she was abreast of him. The woman tilted her face to look at him, told the person on the other end of the phone call to hold on.

"Yes, can I help you?" Her voice held a familiar lilt. American with a touch of undefined foreignness to it. Just like Bailey.

"I don't mean to bother you, but you remind me of someone." Was he really doing this?

"I remind everyone of someone." She laughed, cocking a red-clad hip in challenge.

"Do you know Bailey Hughes?"

The woman's mouth formed an O of surprise. "Yes, I do. She's my sister."

Seven nodded and grinned, glad to know he wasn't going crazy. The woman put the phone back to her ear and told the person on the other end that she would call them back. Black panties flashed as she swung her leg over the white railing between the restaurant and the sidewalk and hopped across the dividing line of red flowers to sit at his table.

"I'm Bette," she said, holding out her hand. "The older one."

He chuckled. "Seven. I was briefly a client of your sister's."

She looked him up and down. Seven felt the heavy weight of her stare as she took in his haircut, clothes, the loafers on his feet.

"You are a cutie, even if your name is a number." She actually peeked under the tablecloth to take a look at *all* of him. "A client, huh? And now what are you?" she asked.

"Interested in becoming much more to her."

"A lover? A BFF? What exactly do you have in mind?

Bailey doesn't have a lot of room in her life for extra, so you have to be sure of what you want with her." She slid her sunglasses up off her face and hooked them in the high nest of her hair.

"Oh, I'm sure about what I want. I just don't want to tell you everything before we can even have a drink together."

Bette signaled the waitress. "Hi, honey. Can you have the bartender mix me up a sidecar, please?"

"Sure thing." The waitress gave her a curious glance as she went to the bartender with the drink order.

Bette sighed and leaned back in her chair. "Another beautiful day in Miami, huh?"

"I don't have any complaints." He reached for his fork to continue his meal.

"Good. Complaints don't change a damn thing anyway."

She dropped her small, shiny purse on the table next to her phone and sunglasses. While she settled herself, Seven continued to eat his food, waiting to see what this interesting version of Bailey had to say once she had that drink. When the waitress returned with a martini glass filled with gold liquid and accented with an orange slice, Bette clapped her hands in happiness. She tasted the sidecar.

"Very nice. Thank you, honey." She turned to Seven. "Now that we've had that drink, tell me everything you want to do to with my sister. In intimate detail." Her eyes danced above the glass as she took another sip.

"You're a demanding one, aren't you?"

"Not really. Bailey is the demanding one. I'm sure you know that already from experience."

Seven nodded. "Yes, she is, and I like that about her."

"That's good. A few guys have been scared off by her over the years. Not that she's trying to have anything serious with some overeager cocker spaniel trying to pee on her stilettos."

Seven paused with his fork halfway to his mouth. "Do I seem overeager?"

"Not especially. What you do seem to me is interesting. Bailey needs interesting. It doesn't matter how much money you have. If you're boring, then she's gone."

The brief thought of Marcus flitted through Seven's mind. He wondered why his friend had never tried to date Bailey. Or had he? Seven had never thought to ask Marcus that question, not until now.

Bette winked across the table at him. "You're the artist, aren't you?"

Seven grinned. Bailey *had* talked to her sister about him. "Yes, I am."

"Good for you. I hope you're not going to give up on her over a little thing like that."

"She gave up on me."

"Do you really think that? No, wait—" She held up her hand, sending her white beaded bangles jangling. "Do you accept that?"

He was far from ready to be with just one woman on a permanent basis, but he was looking forward to spending a bit of time with the intriguing Bailey Hughes. He knew they would have a lot of fun together if she'd just let herself relax and enjoy the possibilities between them.

"No, I don't accept her giving up on me," he said.

"Even better." Bette nodded at him in approval. She plucked a pen and a tiny notebook from her purse, scribbled something down, tore out the page and tucked it under the pepper shaker. "Here's my number if you need help with that."

Seven laughed. "Thanks."

"My pleasure."

Bette reached for her cocktail, drinking deeply from it until it was almost gone. "Listen, I'm not going to hang around all day and chat. I just wanted to see what my sister is into these days."

"Into?"

"A figure of speech." She shrugged.

Seven assumed she was being intentionally vague out of sisterly loyalty. Had Bailey told Bette that she liked him? The thought made him smile. Made him feel generous.

"Would you like something to eat? The salmon-and-asparagus dish here is pretty good."

She looked down at his plate, as if seriously contemplating it. Then she reached for the spoon he hadn't used and scooped out a healthy bite from the salmon. Seven laughed, incredulous.

"Thank you," she said chewing. "That's very sweet of you. A man who shares. I think Bailey will like that." She licked a bit of juice from her lips and smiled back at him.

Seven chuckled. "I meant that I'd buy you lunch."

"No, thanks. I'm not hungry." She plucked an asparagus from his plate and bit into it, nibbling on the green stalk until it was all gone.

She went back to her drink, leaning into the comfortable padded chair to smile at him. Seven liked her. Watching her across the table, he saw again in her what had reminded him so strongly of Bailey. The heart-shaped face and symmetrical mouth. The spare but unique way she had of gesturing when she talked. Her lean gazellelike body. Bette was the more traditional beauty, but Bailey's look was more sensual and earthy.

"Thanks for stopping to chat with me," he said.

"My pleasure. I haven't met anyone my sister has been dating in a long time."

Dating? "Bailey and I aren't dating."

"Yet."

Seven laughed. Yes. He definitely liked Bette.

Chapter 7

Seven sat next to Marcus at a large table in the main room at Gillespie's, enjoying the antics of a birthday party. Seven had sworn he would try to put more distance between himself and the billionaire, but he realized he'd come to like the younger man and even enjoy his company, no matter how outrageous he acted. Tonight, it was all about Nilda Baker, a friend of Marcus's who wanted to buy a sculpture from Seven.

Nilda was as rich as Marcus, but she definitely wasn't as smart about the way she spent her money. She'd just announced that she'd bought an island. In the Arctic. The twenty or so guests gathered at the table applauded, while Seven could only watch in stupefaction. What did a Florida-born woman want with a frozen island thousands of miles from home?

She stood at the head of the table, grinning as she posed for her friend's camera phone. Her bleached-blond hair was stylishly cut, her café au lait skin glowing with achievement as she propped her hands on Gucci-covered hips and laughed at something one of her friends said.

"What are you going to do with this island, Nilda?"

"I'm just going to have it," she said.

The table laughed again.

"Girl, you are ridiculous!" a woman in leather called out teasingly, then joined in on the laughter.

Just then, a waitress came to their table with an accommodating smile. She was gorgeous. Just the type meant to be a waitress, model or trophy wife. Slender body thick in all the right places and shown to perfect advantage in the long-sleeved white shirt, cummerbund and black miniskirt. "Is there anything I can get for you?" she asked Nilda.

Marcus answered for his friend. "Refill all our drinks and bring another round of appetizers."

Apparently the waitress was used to not hearing "please." She nodded, did a visual check around the table, then she pranced away. Marcus watched her walk away with his usual acquisitive leer. None of his latest girls of the moment were there to give him a hard time. Even if they had been, Seven doubted that his host would have cared. They probably would've invited the waitress back with them for a three-or-more-some.

Seven drank the last of his old-fashioned and discreetly moved the glass aside. The music from the club was tight, several low-tempo grooves he hadn't heard before but that went perfectly with the vibe at the table.

Soon, the waitress came back with two other girls behind her. They fanned around the table of twenty, dispensing drinks and appetizers to the appropriate people.

"I didn't order this." One of Marcus's guests pouted. The thick sista with the bouncing Afro waved her hand dismissively at the blue drink in front of her. Everyone knew that was what she had been drinking for the past two hours. Hell, her tongue was blue.

"I sincerely apologize, miss," the waitress said smoothly, picking up the drink and putting it on her empty tray. "What was it that you'd ordered?"

Lorna wanted to make trouble tonight. After her fourth

drink, Seven learned, she was likely to do anything to make the evening livelier. Even if it included making the waitresses miserable.

"I was having Patrón on the rocks."

"Of course, miss." The waitress nodded and straightened. She turned to nod at the other waitresses with her. "I'll have that to you in a few minutes." She smiled at Lorna. "My name is Monique if you need anything else at all tonight."

Lorna didn't even have the grace to look embarrassed. The five glasses of Wild Blue Margarita in her system made her oblivious to her new troublemaker status. Or maybe she just didn't care. Her husband, a thin slam poet–looking guy with a goatee, touched her hand to calm her antics. But Lorna wasn't having it. She flapped him away in irritation. Seven chuckled.

As the waitress backed away from the table, something nearby caught her eye. Her lips parted in the first genuine smile of the night. "Will you be joining their party, miss?"

"Yes, I will."

Seven straightened in his chair at the sound of the unexpected voice. Only a few people at the table turned to see who it was. The slim woman brushed her cheek against Marcus's and signaled for a chair. Bailey. Marcus looked between her and Seven with amusement.

"Put the chair there, please." Bailey pointed to the tiny gap between Marcus and Seven, then moved back to allow the waitress to fit a chair into the small space and encourage everyone to make room for her.

"Thank you." She offered the waitress a smile before claiming the seat, then ordered a Scotch on the rocks.

She didn't have her banker's face on tonight. Or anything else that belonged to a banker, for that matter. This was the first time Seven had ever seen her in a dress. She was the perfect mix of sexy and elegant in the pale blue tube dress, which emphasized the thinness of her body and its subtle curves. Her hair was up again. Swept high to the top of her head in a coronet of curls. Her lipstick was bright red. So were the nails Seven saw briefly through her peep-toe shoes. Her fingernails shone with clear polish. The only touch of the banker.

Up close, her bared shoulders glimmered with a dusting of luminescent powder. He curled his hands on the table against the urge to touch her skin. Was she as soft as she looked? A hint of scent, something crisp and citrusy, flowed to him from her skin.

Without a word, she had undone him. Did she regret her last words to him in her office a few days ago? It was the weekend now. Was she ready to let her banker's guard down and take a chance on him?

"You smell very edible," he said.

She glanced at him through the thick fringe of her lashes, another creature entirely from the one he'd seen last.

"There's no taste test," she replied with a faint smile.

Seven grinned. She was here to play.

"I was very distraught after our last encounter." He turned to face her, ignoring Marcus's amused and curious gaze on the other side of her. "You broke my heart."

She continued to look at him, then slowly she reached up and touched his chest through the red polo shirt. He swore she must have felt his heart racing under her palm.

"You seem to be in one piece," she said.

"Cruel woman."

"Not at all. I'm the sweet pussycat everyone wishes they had."

Seven's hips twitched in the seat. He didn't know whether to fling her hand away from him or pull her closer. She solved his dilemma by removing her hand, dropping it to the table to finger the long cylindrical shape of the wrapped utensils the waitress had left for her next to a clean plate.

He cleared his throat. "So, are you here to celebrate Nilda's island, too?"

"Yes, she promised if I showed up she'd name it after me."

Seven chuckled. "I think she might have misled you on that one. Early on, someone mentioned it's now officially called Nilda's Isle."

"How original," she murmured.

"Not everyone can be as clever as you, Ms. Hughes."

"True."

He laughed. Then sobered. It was hard to forget how they had left things, her throwing him out of her office because of his job. His disappointment when she'd let the spark of what they could have had die so easily. Then there had been that glimpse of her that evening at the beach. He swore that when he'd looked up to the top of the low-rise building, she had been there. A softly glowing light above him.

"So have you decided to forgive me for my job?"

"No. I told you, I'm not here for you. Nilda and her island requested my company and I am here. But—" she pursed her lips "—I would like to talk with you about something before you leave tonight."

Hope lurched awake in his chest. "We can talk right now."

"I don't think so. Later."

Just then, the waitress returned with drinks, leaning over to serve Bailey hers before placing Lorna's troublesome drink in front of her. "Let me know if you need anything else," the waitress said. She looked at Bailey as if she knew her or maybe wanted to. Bailey rewarded her with a smile.

"Tell me, what really brought you here tonight?" Seven

would have loved to hear her say the words, say that it was the possibility of seeing him that had brought her out of her tower to mix with the common folk.

But she only smiled coyly at him again. She raised her voice. "Congratulations on your island purchase, Nilda. I hear some Canadian almost got the jump on you during the bidding."

The golden birthday girl twirled in her organza dress to face Bailey. She tilted her head. "How did you know that?"

Bailey shrugged. "You know how Miami is. Everyone knows everything two minutes after you do it."

"Ain't that the truth!" someone else at the table said.

"Thanks for the congrats, Bailey. I didn't know if you'd show up. We rarely see you out."

Seven thought he saw a touch of color on Bailey's cheeks. "To break up the routine. You know how it is."

Nilda laughed. In the past few days, Seven had learned that Nilda's routine wasn't much of one. She wasn't bound to a job, a man, a schedule, or anyone else, for that matter. She invested well, played hard and always picked up the check. And now she wanted to buy something of Seven's.

Bailey leaned back in her chair between Seven and Marcus.

"I think we're all surprised to see you out tonight," Marcus said. "Surprised and delighted, of course. Your brand of hotness always makes any party better." He spread it on thick with his usual megawatt smile.

The look on Bailey's face said she wasn't buying what he was selling. "Flatterer" was all she said.

After taking a few sips from her drink, bantering back and forth with Marcus, Bailey touched his arm. "Can I see you outside for a moment?"

Seven didn't hesitate. "Of course." He stood up and waited for her to do the same. "After you."

With one last sip of her Scotch, she left the table and led the way out to the terrace overlooking the hectic street. Seven didn't restrain himself from watching her alluring body in that pale blue dress. The body-hugging material allowed for the rhythmic shift of her behind, showed off the startling clarity of the dark skin of her shoulders and arms. Watching her was like listening to a particular, sensual song. He felt wrapped up in her, seduced into her. And Seven didn't want to get free.

Chapter 8

Bailey hated what she was doing. The partners had decreed that Seven Carmichael would be good for the company, so here she was like a good little employee, getting them what she needed. And it didn't help that she wanted to be here. The most intimate and female part of her wanted to flirt with Seven and touch his chest again and invite him away from this ridiculous crowd to eat hamburgers, drink beer and watch the sunrise from the beach. She wanted those things so badly with him that she could almost taste them. Bailey bit the inside of her cheek.

The balcony just outside the main room was already occupied. A few couples. A lone woman smoking a cigar. Some twentysomethings giggling over photos on an iPhone they passed between themselves. Not unusual for a Friday night at one of the most popular clubs in Miami.

As Bailey had come in, there was already a line at the door extending well beyond the velvet rope. The only reason she'd gotten past the usually fair doorman was because she claimed to be a member of Marcus's party. A party she had no desire to count herself a number of. All she had wanted tonight was Seven.

Bailey turned to him as he came up behind her. Quiet, graceful, his eyes following every movement of her body in the dress. She felt warmed by him. An artist? Really?

Sometimes, the universe was too cruel. But she wouldn't suspend her principles over a pretty face. Or a nice body. Seven came closer to her as she leaned back against the cool metal railing. A really nice body.

He smelled like that same cologne from before, clean like a forest at dawn. When she was a little girl, her parents had taken her and Bette into a rain forest in Brazil. The tall trees and moss-strewn trails had filled her with a sense of awe even as the smell of the forest, like healthy and growing things, had comforted her and made her want to stay. Seven smelled like that.

Bailey held up her hand to prevent him from coming closer. Like in the club before, her palm rested against his chest. A solid warmth that made her want to snuggle close and bite.

"Stop," she said. But her voice was weak.

He stopped.

"What do you want to talk to me about?"

Bailey swallowed, hoping he didn't notice her hesitation. "Not this," she said.

"What?" But he was smiling. Resting under the weak restraint of her hand against his chest while he looked down at her as if he wanted to peel her clothes off and taste every inch of her. Bailey swallowed again. She would let him. If that was what he wanted, she would let him.

"I don't want to pursue anything with you," she said. "At least not romantically." She noticed his devouring look again. "Or sexually."

He seemed to grow harder under her hand. "Okay. Tell me."

"I want you to become a client at the firm."

"Okay. I will."

"What?" She blinked in surprise.

"I'll become your client. That's what you want, isn't it?"

"Yes, but…" Why had it been so easy?

"I think it's only fair that I warn you about something." He paused to push closer, closing the space between them until her hand was caught between their bodies. "I want you." Seven braced his arms on either side of her on the railing, pressing his scent into her, his heavy intention. "And I'm not going to stop until I have you."

Her knees turned to jelly at his words. But she had never been that type of woman. Macho statements like that only had the effect of turning her off, of making her push back even harder. The problem was, even though his words were confident, they weren't macho. Simply a statement of fact. Bailey bit the inside of her cheek, but said nothing.

"I already told you, nothing can happen between us, Seven."

"I know what you told me, but you don't believe that."

"You are—" She gestured to him, difficult as it was with him pressed against her body. "You're not what I want in my life."

"But how do you know I'm not what you need?" His breath smelled of whiskey and oranges.

"I don't need some kind of artist in my life. I don't need Marcus and his friends pushing up in my personal business. I don't need drama."

The corner of Seven's mouth quirked up. "I'm not offering drama." He moved slightly back, giving her the barest amount of room to breathe. "I'm offering you this." And he dipped his head.

His mouth hovered over hers for a moment, giving her the chance to back away, to withdraw from the kiss they both knew was coming. But Bailey did not pull away. She would have been a hypocrite to deny she had been curious about the feel of his mouth. *What harm would it do?*

a small voice asked as his lips pressed against hers. Their flesh touched. Sweet. His kiss was sweet.

She sighed. He pressed closer. He moved his mouth against hers, a steady warm pressure that she gladly returned. Her mouth tingled. Her body moved into his. Her arms lifted to sweep around his neck. The sweetness overwhelmed her, made her sigh again. Seven licked her mouth, tasted her lipstick, then the delicate insides of her mouth. Kissed her more deeply until the sweetness ended and passion began. He slanted his mouth over hers and she dove into the kiss with him, parting her lips, lifting up on tiptoe to meet his strength and the hot intrusion of his tongue as it swept into her mouth, tasting every inch of her inside, licking, tasting, until Bailey moaned into him, clung tighter, dug her fingernails into the back of his neck.

A delicate, rippling sweat blossomed under her clothes as her entire body blushed for him. A thickness settled between her thighs, and she wanted to shove his hand there. Her nipples tingled against her dress. She moaned again.

The sound of giggling abruptly penetrated her fog of passion. The twentysomethings who had been circulating the cell phone had found something else to entertain them. Bailey wouldn't have been surprised to find a camera phone directed at her and Seven. She stiffened and pulled away from him, breathing heavily. His breath was none too steady, either. That made her feel better. A blush heated her face, and she turned abruptly away from him to face the evening beyond the balcony.

She wanted to… She needed… Images of what she wanted came to her. Hot. Clawing. Sweaty. Impossible. She squeezed her eyes shut, pressed a hand over her racing heart. Seven stood just behind her, but she couldn't face him yet. He would easily see the hunger in her face. See how effortless it would be for her to forget her precious principles and make love with him tonight.

"If it makes you feel better, you can tell yourself that kiss was to seal our new business arrangement." His breath brushed the back of her neck. "I'll see you in your office on Monday."

A hot tremor quaked her thighs. She fought it and straightened, then turned around, determined to reclaim her composure and get back on even footing with Seven. But, except for the whispering girls and the woman smoking her cigar, Bailey was alone. She swallowed her disappointment, then turned back to the night, hoping it would soothe her riotous mind and overheated body.

Chapter 9

It felt different to be in her office and know what her mouth tasted like.

Seven sat in one of the chairs across the desk from Bailey, the same chair he'd sat in a week before, with one thing on his mind: how to get Bailey to be herself with him.

He'd seen glimpses of the real Bailey that first day he visited her in her office, but from the time she decided he wasn't the man for her, she'd withdrawn from him. A half hour before, he'd walked into her office and signed all the necessary papers for him to officially become a client of her firm, given her everything she needed, and still she stayed aloof from him. In some way he thought it would be better, different at least, now that they knew what the other tasted like. For him, the difference was clear. Now, more than ever, he was sure he wanted her to be his woman. But, it seemed she was really convinced he was the wrong man for her.

But he kept reliving their kiss. He'd never felt anything like it before. The breath-shaking lust that had ripped through him at her touch had nearly brought him to his knees. In those precious minutes, he'd nearly gone mad with desire for her. If they hadn't been in such a public place, or if any more of his control had slipped away, he would have shoved up her dress and buried himself inside her. And she would have let him. He'd seen that answering desire in her face.

Then she had turned away from him as if she'd regretted touching him. Well, he had no time for regrets. Only for getting what he wanted. And he wanted Bailey Hughes.

Across the desk from him, she was cool as an alpine breeze. Beautiful again in that untouchable way, her banker's mask on, her high heels firmly on the ground. She typed something into her slim desktop computer.

"We're almost done," she said. As if he'd fidgeted or she wanted him gone.

He watched her over the steeple of his fingers, enjoying the view. "I'm comfortable. I don't have any plans for the afternoon."

Actually, he did have plans to check out a studio space in Wynwood, but it was something that could wait if she wanted to keep him longer. And he was very open to her keeping him as long as she wanted.

As Bailey put his financial life in her sleek little work machine, Seven plotted. He dreamed. He watched her thin fingers fly over the keyboard, the way the light from the window shadowed her short lashes against her cheekbones, the subtle rise and fall of the high-necked gray blouse over her chest.

"Marcus is having a party on his boat," he said.

Bailey flicked her gaze briefly his way. "That's nothing new. That man looks for excuses to have a party."

"This is something special. It's some charity to benefit orphans. He'd like you to be there on behalf of Braithwaite and Fernandez, maybe give a donation."

"Marcus? Involved in a charity?" She sounded incredulous, then she chuckled and shook her head. "I guess he's desperate for a write-off this year."

"Whatever the reason, he wants you there. It's a week-

end afternoon thing, so you don't have to worry about missing work."

She chuckled again. "I'll think about it. I've gone to
too many of Marcus's parties lately. I'm sure he's getting
downright suspicious of my motives."

"Does he think you're trying to get into my pants?"
Seven raised a teasing brow. "If not, you're more than welcome to make it seem that way when we're together. Touch
me. Kiss me. Whatever your pleasure." He leaned back in
his chair, watching her try not to laugh. He loved the way
her nose crinkled when she thought something was funny,
even if she didn't laugh right away.

She pressed her lips together, trying to hide a smile.
Behind the rectangular wire-rimmed glasses, her eyes
twinkled. "I think Marcus already has enough assumptions about you and me running around his head. I won't
feed him any more."

"He doesn't need anyone to feed him anything. He car-
ries on full speed ahead anyway. Like this charity thing.
Just say you'll come so he'll leave me alone about it. You
don't want him to harass your client, do you?"

Bailey looked up at him, made a few strokes on her keyboard, then leaned back in her chair. The printer behind
her purred and began spitting out documents. "Fine, I'll
come. But I can't donate more than two thousand dollars
in the firm's name. That's our cap on unverified charities."
Her smile threatened again. She stood up and gathered the
printed documents, then tucked them into a manila envelope.

"Thank you," Seven said. "I'll pass along the good
news."

"The other good news is that you're done here." She
slid the manila envelope across the desk to Seven. "Here

are copies of the documents you signed earlier, with your scanned signature. You're all set."

"You're very efficient." Seven stood up, almost laughing at the expression of disbelief on her face at his easy capitulation to this being a business-only meeting. He picked up the envelope and reached across the desk to shake her hand. "I'll see you again soon," he said.

"All right."

She stood up to walk him to the door, statuesque in her five-inch heels and with her hair once again parted down the middle and conservatively styled.

Seven opened the door and stepped out into the hallway.

"Have a good rest of the day," she said.

"I definitely will." He nodded in her direction and headed for the elevators, forcing himself not to look back at her framed in the doorway of her office.

Bailey was a bright light, but she kept herself on a low burn to please others, to do what she thought she should. Seven intended to take the damper off her light and show her what it was like to burn out of control.

Chapter 10

Bailey dressed carefully the day of Marcus's charity boat party. She tried to tell herself it wasn't because Seven was going to be there—was he really going to be there?—but because she wanted to represent the firm well. The second time she passed by the mirror to make sure her push-up bra was doing its job, she had to face the hard fact: homeless kids didn't care about her cleavage.

The *Dirty Diana* bobbed gracefully at the dock of Marcus's mansion. As Bailey walked through the mostly quiet rear grounds and made her way toward the boat, she wondered where everyone was. A charity wasn't very successful if people weren't there to give money. Maybe she'd give the charity an extra two thousand dollars from her own bank account.

"Bailey girl!" Marcus called out from somewhere on the boat. "Why am I not surprised that you're on time?"

She heard his voice but couldn't see him. "How long have you known me?" she asked, walking closer.

A few seconds later, Marcus appeared on deck in boat shoes, khaki Dockers pants and a flame-red polo shirt. "You look like a hot mama! How are the homeless orphans going to resist that?"

He chuckled, leering in his usual way at her breasts propped up in the neckline of the yellow tank top, and the dazzle of the dozen or so slender gold chains shimmering against her cleavage and down to the middle of her belly. To offset the cleavage, she'd worn jeans and sunflower-colored heels.

"You are a pig, Marcus. Are you sure you're having this charity for homeless kids, or is this another way for you to find more women to sleep with?" She grabbed the railing of the ramp and made her careful way aboard the boat.

"I don't need to find women, baby. They find me."

There was no denying that. Women were drawn to Marcus like pigs to a full trough. He was attractive enough, she supposed. And having all that money at his disposal was always a draw. But he was just always doing too much. On the boat, she greeted him with a kiss on the cheek, pulling away first when he held on to her a little bit too long.

"Where is everybody?"

"They're coming, but that doesn't stop the show. Come on." He took her hand and led her belowdecks to the plush salon of the eighty-foot yacht.

It had been a long time since Bailey had been aboard the boat. Each time, the luxury of it took her breath away. Gleaming cherry walls everywhere she looked, big-screen TVs in nearly every room and, where she stood, a wide-open salon with windows to let in the light and the view of the beautiful water all around them. Now the white curtains over the windows were closed, allowing in the brightness of the day without the distraction of the beauty that lay outside.

Marcus beckoned. "Come into the dining room."

Bailey followed, remembering from a tour he'd given her a few years before that the yacht had three bedrooms fitted with queen-size beds, plus a few other places to bunk if a guest wasn't too fussy.

On a table against one wall of the dining room sat a

platter of hors d'oeuvres and a bucket filled with ice and a bottle of champagne. Babyface sang "When Can I See You Again?" from the stereo. All the windows in the dining room, except for a small porthole, were also covered.

"Make yourself comfortable, baby. Put down your purse and relax. The party is just about to start." Marcus grinned. "The little kiddies are going to be so happy you dropped by."

Just to be contrary, Bailey gripped her purse more tightly under her arm. Marcus shrugged and adjusted the champagne in the bucket, picked up a shrimp from the hors d'oeuvres tray and popped it into his mouth. The mini tray of food looked good, especially since she hadn't eaten all morning, having gotten up late from an all-night gab session with Bette to gulp down a glass of orange juice before she left her sister to fend for herself at her condo.

She was surprised at the healthy variety of food: tiny empanadas, mini Italian salads, golden grilled shrimp curled around pegs of wilted garlic, and cubes of various cheeses. All things that she liked. It wasn't enough to feed an entire party of folks, though. Bailey tucked her clutch under her arm and took one of the tiny caprese salads, a basil leaf cupped around a cherry tomato and a ball of mozzarella. It was perfectly seasoned, with the basil a fresh burst of flavor in her mouth. A delicious counterpoint to the olive oil, bits of ground pepper and sea salt.

She looked up from the hors d'oeuvre tray to see Marcus watching her with a strange look on his face.

"What?"

"Nothing. Just, damn, you look fine today."

Bailey laughed. "Thanks. But don't start that again."

Years ago, when they'd met at a Miami Fashion Week party, Marcus thought he wanted her. At least he said so often enough that he might have believed it, following her around the party and sending drink after drink her way until she'd finally agreed to go on a date with him. She thought they'd go to The Grove and have a nice dinner, some drinks, maybe catch a play. Instead, he'd shown up at her condo in a limousine and swept her off to the airport. They'd taken a private plane to New Orleans—during one of their brief conversations, she'd told him she loved Cajun food—and had dinner at a small restaurant not too far from the French Quarter.

His show of wealth had impressed her at first, but he couldn't stop talking about what he could do for her. And that turned her off.

She'd waited until they were back in Miami and a day had passed before she let him know she wasn't interested in anything more than friendship with him. He had been surprised and, she thought, insulted. But a few days later, she'd seen him at another party romancing identical twin models.

He'd called her over to share a table and a round of drinks with them. Maybe he thought she'd be jealous and decline the invitation out of pique. But she'd sashayed right on over and had martinis with them, even gotten the twins' numbers, because they were interested in diversifying their funds and making their modeling money work for them when they didn't feel like working anymore.

Since that day, Marcus had seemed to take a strange sort of pleasure in recommending Bailey and her firm to his friends. It was mostly because of the big-name clients he referred that her bosses at Braithwaite and Fernandez Wealth Management started seriously considering her for partnership.

On the yacht, Marcus speared a mini empanada with a toothpick and bit into it. "I'm not starting a thing with you, girl. Just appreciating how nice you look."

"Thank you." Bailey smiled and turned away from him.

If this was how the rest of this party was going to be, she was going to have to leave early. She looked at her watch.

"No worries! I'm not trying to bother you. Chill." A noise from up on deck made him look toward the stairs. "Anyway, I have to get going. See you later." He grabbed the banister and ran up the stairs.

Moments later, Bailey heard him talking with someone, another man. Then quick footsteps overhead walking away. Masculine feet in white Converse shoes appeared on the first step. Then brown legs, plaid cargo shorts and a white T-shirt draped over a muscular chest. Seven.

"You do look sexy," he said by way of greeting. "Damn!"

He came all the way down the stairs and into the salon, a devilish smile on display, and greeted her with a quick kiss on the cheek. "Did you eat?"

She got the chance to only briefly touch his bare arm to return the salutation before he drew away to open the refrigerator and take out a bottle of water. He smelled fresh, as if he'd just gotten out of the shower. No cologne today.

An image of him in the shower flashed in her mind before she could stop it. Water raining down his muscular back, swirling over the firm muscles of his buttocks and thighs. Bailey's heart lurched in her chest. She touched the table behind her for balance. Despite her resolution, her body couldn't help but react to him.

"I…uh…yes, I had some of this stuff." She gestured to the platter of finger foods.

"Well, make a plate. You probably haven't even eaten today. I picked these up trying to guess what you'd like to eat." He twisted off the cap to the water and put the bottle to his mouth.

Bailey watched the motion of his throat, the strong neck, suddenly thirsty herself. When he took the bottle from his mouth, she reached out for it. After a moment's hesitation he gave it to her. She drank deeply from the bottle, sucking the cool water down her throat, slaking the sudden and overwhelming thirst until the bottle was nearly empty. When she took it from her mouth, Seven had a strange smile on his face.

"I bet you're hungry, too," he said. "Sit with me and we can eat and drink together." He took the bottle from her, got another from the refrigerator and picked up two plates.

As he stepped away, Bailey regained her equilibrium. She looked outside the porthole and saw the boat was moving. It hadn't been his nearness, after all. Wait a minute! Why…?

"We're moving!"

She ran to take a closer look outside, kneeling on the padded leather bench at the dining room table to peer out the face-sized porthole. Marcus's palm-tree-flanked mansion was slowly falling behind the *Dirty Diana*. Blue water rippled like a ribbon between the boat and the dock, the few yards of separation threatening to quickly become a mile.

"Of course," Seven said. "This is a boat, after all."

He prepared two plates of food, grabbed the bottles of water and joined her on the bench.

But Bailey didn't understand. Weren't they waiting for everyone else to show up?

Seven shoved a full plate in front of her along with a bottle of water. "Eat. It's going to be a long day and you'll need your strength."

"What are you talking about? What's going on here?"

He watched her with a strange look on his face, expectant, almost nervous. He took another sip of his water.

"I'm kidnapping you," he said.

Chapter 11

Bailey's mouth dropped open, stayed open for an embarrassing number of seconds. "What?"

"I'm kidnapping you," Seven repeated. He put a grilled shrimp in his mouth and chewed.

Bailey jumped up from the bench to one of the covered windows in the dining room. She wrenched away the covering. And could see in wide blue-and-white Technicolor that there was no one on Marcus's dock but her former friend, who was watching the departing boat, hands shoved in his pockets, the breeze fluttering his clothes. After a moment, he turned and walked down the pier toward the house.

"What the hell?" She let the curtain fall back and stood up to confront Seven. "Take me back right now! This is ridiculous. This is illegal!"

Her heart knocked hard in her chest. As she looked at him, the slow way he ate his food, and he stared at her with a blatant unconcern for what she would do next, she realized that she wasn't really frightened. She was furious!

"This is bull—"

"No need to get upset," he interrupted. "Just think of this as a vacation. Your sister knows where you are, and Marcus does, too. The boat will bring you back here safe and sound in a few days."

Bailey's head spun with the sudden facts. Bette knew about this. They'd be gone for a few days.

Days?

She spun away from him, dashing from the dining room, through the salon, up the stairs to the deck and up to the pilothouse. She wrenched open the door. The man behind the wheel of the boat looked at her with a question in his face. His copilot continued reading instruments and making notes on a pad as if she wasn't there.

"Can I help you, miss?" the pilot asked.

"I'm being kidnapped. I demand to be taken home immediately." She knew she sounded like the melodramatic heroine from a bad movie, but she was desperate to have this farce over with.

"I'm sorry, miss. Mr. Stanfield gave us strict orders."

"And what exactly are those orders?"

"To stick to the itinerary Mr. Carmichael gave us."

Beyond the pilothouse, Marcus's mansion drifted even farther away. They passed other docks on Star Island, making their way out of Biscayne Bay, toward the sea.

"This is not legal!" Bailey was so angry she could scream. If she stayed there any longer talking to the pilot, she was going to start shouting some very rude things. She clenched her fist against her thigh, helplessness adding to her fury. A virulent curse blasted past her lips.

The copilot looked up. "I'm afraid you'll have to go to Mr. Carmichael for that, miss."

Feeling defeated, Bailey walked back toward the dining room, feeling the weight of every single step she took from the pilothouse, barely noticing the wind that brushed tenderly against her face, the sweet salt taste of the air. As she approached the stairs leading belowdecks, she straightened her spine. Her mother hadn't raised any weak children, and she'd be damned if she showed any weakness to Seven Carmichael.

"You know this is some bull, right?" she said once she reached the dining room.

"No, this is a vacation." He sprawled on the bench with the remnants of his meal on the table, water bottle held loosely in his hand. "The firm doesn't need you right now—" He held up a hand to stall her beginning protest. "Your sister checked. It's all cool. Nothing you can't handle when you return."

Everything had seemed to be getting back to neutral. When he had accepted their purely business relationship the last time they met at her office, a small part of her had been disappointed. But she knew she should have been relieved. He had been so nonchalant about the platonic turn their relationship had taken. And the entire time he had been planning this. This!

It was one thing to bring a picnic lunch into her office, but this was so much more.

"You're going to regret this," she said, ice crystallizing in her voice.

"I might. But I'd regret it even more if I didn't try." He took a drink of his water. "A woman like you doesn't allow for small gestures. It's either go big or go home. And I'm only going home if I take you with me."

His words plunged the room into silence as Bailey stared at him in disbelief. *Is this man serious?*

"Please. This is the twenty-first century, not the damn Dark Ages." Bailey rocked back on one leg, cocking her hip to look at him. In that moment, she realized she still held her yellow clutch under her arm. Feeling ridiculous, she crossed her arms over her chest, not giving him any sign of her weakness.

"I know. Maybe I shouldn't have said *kidnap,* then." He

chuckled ruefully and shook his head. "This is, I hope, a more elegant enterprise than that."

Now it was Bailey's turn to shake her head. "Elegant? You are out of your damn mind."

"You've bewitched me." He smiled crookedly.

Bailey watched as he pulled the curtains back from the windows, revealing their seaward journey from the waters of Biscayne Bay toward the Caribbean.

If Seven had tried to touch her, she would have fought— hell, she would have jumped off the boat and swum for the dock—but he only pulled open each curtain until the dining room and adjoining salon were filled with light and the view of the Miami skyline passing by.

He moved with a lean, slow grace she was coming to enjoy more and more. He didn't rush, he teased the air with his presence, eased his big body into movements that were like a dance. She shook her head again. *Idiot. Why don't you just go ahead and thank him for kidnapping you, then?*

"Relax," he said without turning around. "I won't force you to do anything you don't want."

Too late. Already, against what she wanted, against what she needed, she was sinking into the pleasure of being with him. His easy tone, his beauty, the goodness of the man she could slowly see he was—all these things were wearing away at her anger.

Bailey threw her purse down on the table. The yellow leather slid across the polished cherrywood and dropped into the bench where Seven had sat before.

"Don't think I'm going to make this easy for you," she said.

He finally looked at her. "I'm counting on you not to." His voice was rough, a delicious caress.

Damn.

Chapter 12

Seven was worried. Bailey's anger was something he had been prepared for in the abstract, but facing the alternating freezing cold and blazing heat in her eyes, he worried that his errand was that of a fool. She was gorgeous in her righteous anger. If he hadn't been so desperate for her to see him as himself instead of what she assumed, Seven didn't know if he would have done this. Kidnapped her. Damn, it sounded so harsh when she said it.

She stood in front of him, her pose confrontational— arms crossed and hip cocked to one side. Sexy as hell. Seven only barely stopped his eyes from wandering where they wanted. But he'd long ago perfected the art of the full-body scan without overtly moving his eyes. He did it again and had to swallow hard.

He wanted her. He wanted her more than he'd ever wanted any other woman in his life. Challenge, beauty, sex appeal. Not to mention the kiss they'd shared the other night, which almost melted his shorts. She was coming to mean more to him than he expected, more than what made him comfortable. Seven stood up.

"Come have a drink with me. Marcus left champagne."

She cocked her chin and leaned even farther back on her hip. Challenging. Scornful. "What am I going to do on this boat with nothing to wear for days?" Her tone suggested how much of an idiot he was.

"You can just walk around naked," he suggested with a restrained leer.

She made a dismissive noise. "In your dreams."

"Oh, yes."

She looked at him. He grinned back with a shrug. "Sue me. I have very vivid dreams about you. Almost every night."

Bailey made the same noise again, plucked off her shoes and tucked them side by side against the wall. The loss of her heels immediately brought her within closer reach, made her seem vulnerable in a way she hadn't been before. "I can't wear this outfit every day," she said.

She dropped down on the bench next to him, keeping at least two feet of space between them.

"What's wrong with it?" He used the question as an excuse to examine her body in a more direct way.

The yellow tank top clung to her slim torso. The lacy edge of a pink bra peeked out from the neckline with its wealth of cleavage. Her plump, deep brown skin seduced his eyes more than once. Seven looked his fill now with hot appreciation, eyes falling to the figure-hugging jeans and her bare feet with the toes painted blue.

She put her feet up on the chair across from her, allowing his stare. "Well?"

"I want to make love to you." His throat caught. That wasn't what he'd meant to say.

From the look on Bailey's face, his words had caught her by surprise, too. But he wouldn't apologize for them. He meant every single one.

"I'm going outside," she said, and abruptly stood up, heading out to the salon and up the stairs.

Her bare feet slapped against the wooden stairs as she hurried away.

"Idiot."

He cursed himself with a few more choice words before taking a deep breath. Okay, if he hadn't scared her away before now, that definitely did the job. Seven took a step toward the stairs. He should go to her. And say what? That he was sorry? That he didn't want to sink his face into her soft breasts and touch her until she screamed his name? That would be a lie. He clenched his jaw.

Leave her alone already, man. He could practically hear Marcus's voice in his ear, calling him a hundred kinds of fool.

When he'd first come up with the plan, Marcus had laughed in his face.

"She's going to cut you off at the knees!" he had said with way too much satisfaction. "That chick will rip your stones out and feed them to you before you sail past Key Biscayne."

"Fine, I'll share them with her for a snack. Will you lend me your boat or what?"

"Of course. I just wish I had a video camera on board so I could see you crash and burn." Marcus had laughed again. "But, seriously, do you think this is the smartest thing to do? This chick is a raptor. You may think you're ready for her claws, but you're not."

With such a ringing endorsement, Seven had put the rest of his plan in motion, including contacting her sister about calling in on Bailey's behalf at work. The woman had been more than happy to help, barely holding back her laughter as she told him how much her sister needed a long, hard "vacation."

Seven had pushed to get what he wanted: Bailey here with him on the boat. Now it was time for him to ease off. They both needed time to get used to this new and potentially volatile situation.

* * *

Seven checked to make sure her room was ready, that it had everything she needed, before going up to the pilot-house and talking to the crew. They already had their instructions about where they were going and how fast to get there, but he wanted to make sure they were on course and on time. He didn't want to get to their destination too late, or even too early. Then he went out on deck.

The boat had picked up speed as it left the skyscrapers of downtown Miami behind. The impressive twist of highways against the tropical blue sky, the beaches, barely dressed bronzed, gold, brown and black bodies basking in the sunshine. The *Dirty Diana* cut through the water like a blade, heading south. There were other boaters on the water, and some waved at Seven as he made his way up to the sundeck with the wind flapping at his clothes and bringing a squint to his eyes. He plucked his sunglasses from the pocket of his shorts and put them on. Water occasionally splashed up to sprinkle coolness against his face and bare arms as he walked.

Deliberately, he did not look for Bailey. Instead, he climbed up to the very top of the luxury yacht, stripped off everything except his swimming trunks and spread himself out on a blanket under the sun. He sighed as his body relaxed against the deck.

Growing up, his parents used to encourage his and his brother's love of the sun. So many families around them had tried to protect the brown and yellow complexions of their children by keeping them out of the sun. His father had worked outside with his hands as a landscaper and had maintained a thriving garden of his own, and his mother had been a nurse. She'd made sure to put sunscreen on her two boys before allowing their brown skin under the UV rays, but she never bothered them about dark skin or light skin. Seven sometimes wondered if things would have been the same if they had been girls. Soon, he closed his eyes and dozed.

"Don't you look relaxed?"

He blinked the sleep from his eyes to see Bailey crouched next to him. She didn't look relaxed.

"I have another blanket if you want to share." He raised his voice above the sound of the high wind from the boat's flight and patted the deck beside him.

She scowled but he could see that her heart wasn't in it.

"Just relax." He was sure he'd said that to her at least half a dozen times already. And that it had had the opposite of its desired effect.

For a moment, she said nothing, only crouched next to him with the open sky around her, white clouds in the vast blue, her yellow shirt turning her into a bright sun above him. Her hair blew wildly in the wind.

"You shouldn't have done this," she finally said. "Nothing good can come out of this trip."

"Well, maybe I can at least get a good tan."

She squinted down at him, taking in his body in a matter-of-fact way, lingering at his chest, his stomach and his hips. His skin tingled beneath her regard, and for a moment, he thought he would embarrass himself. Very casually, he turned over, presenting his back to the sun and hiding the growing evidence of his arousal.

"Time to give my back some sun time," he said over his shoulder.

She smirked. Then, after another considering look at him, she pulled off her shirt and wriggled out of her jeans. "I might as well take advantage of the sun myself. Nothing wrong with a good tan."

He shook his head. "Not fair."

"What's not fair?" She looked like innocence itself as

she lay back on the bare deck, arching her breasts, covered in pink lace and a glittering curtain of tiny gold chains that blew back against her skin in the high wind.

"Tease." He reached out and she stiffened, giving him a poisonous glance that let him know—if her little strip tease wasn't sign enough—what plan she had put into motion to fight him back: Operation Blue Balls.

"Your clothes," he said. They were gripped in her fist to save them from being carried off by the high wind generated by the boat's swift journey on the water. "I'll put them there." He nodded to the small storage container behind them.

She flushed, then let him have the clothes. With what he thought was admirable skill, he was able to open the container and drop her clothes in without her seeing the evidence of his desire for her. He almost high-fived himself. In times like these, it was the small victories that counted the most.

"This is what you wanted, wasn't it? Me naked and at your mercy?"

"You naked, in good time. At my mercy, never." Seven shook his head. "You have clothes waiting for you in the master stateroom. Your sister made good use of my credit card. If there's something wrong with the clothes, blame her."

"How did you get Bette to go along with this? You could be a mass murderer, for all she knows."

"She said I was too sexy to be a mass murderer." Seven laughed, remembering their conversation. Bailey didn't look amused. "She said you need a vacation." He shrugged. "That's the reason I think she went along with it. You've been burning yourself out trying to get the promotion at work. It's not healthy." Seven saw her disgusted expression. "Bette's words, not mine." But he agreed.

Staying at work all the daylight hours was fine to get a project done, but when it was every day, it didn't bode well for work/life balance. And Seven wanted her to have a good balance so she could fit him into her life.

"Your sister loves you," he said. "She just wants you to have a little fun."

"Bette thinks all of life is fun."

"Isn't it?"

"Not for me." Bailey squinted against the bright sun and turned to face him.

"That's a very, very sad thing to hear, Ms. Hughes."

Seven held her gaze for a moment, trying to ignore the intoxicating nearness of her half-naked body, the way the hot sun brought beads of sweat to the surface of her skin, making it glow. Then he gave up. He swept her form with what he knew was a hungry look. "You should go and see about those clothes in your room. I'm not an uncontrollable beast, but I'm not made of stone, either."

Chapter 13

Bailey was going to strangle Bette next time she saw her. She left Seven on deck, sunning himself, and went to find the bedroom he had set aside for her. The boat was big, but the directions he gave her were clear enough. A folded piece of pink paper with her name on it was taped to the door. Bailey plucked it off the door and went inside the room.

As promised, an overnight bag sat on the bed. One of hers from college. The one Bette always tried to borrow when she went off on one of her "hoe trips." She upended the red leather bag on the bed and nearly groaned at the lack of real clothes her sister had bought for her.

"You are dead, Bette Hughes. So freaking dead."

Everything in the bag still had tags attached. There were several thin sundresses, two pairs of strappy flat sandals, a tiny orange bikini and other questionable items of clothing that Bailey wouldn't normally wear. Bandeau tops. Short skirts. Sexy lingerie. Bette's only concession to Bailey's tastes were two pairs of shorts that came to midthigh and their matching tank tops, her iPod, curling iron and hair products. Underneath the iPod was a box of condoms.

"Dammit, Bette!"

She shoved the condoms back in the bag along with everything else. Growling in frustration, she sank into the bed. Why was this girl intent on ruining her life? The piece of paper she'd taken from the door crinkled under her. She plucked it from under her butt and opened it.

Hey, sis!
I know you want to kill me, but so sad for you, I'm a few hundred miles away by now. You may even want to kill that gorgeous guy who brought you out on that boat. Don't. Your life has been shrinking too much in the past few years, especially after Clive. Stop the madness! Do more fun and spontaneous stuff. I'm not saying turn into me now (laughing!) but enjoy all that money you've been saving. Enjoy your life.
Have some sex and live! XOX
—Bette

Bailey refolded the piece of pink paper and gently tucked it in the side of her bag. She sighed. There was nothing wrong with the way she did things now. She saved. She worked hard and she never had to worry about being homeless or someone leaving her alone when she most needed them. But she knew a weak protest when she heard it.

Clive. She sighed again. She hadn't consciously thought about her past with Clive in forever. He was a nice guy. Cute. But she honestly couldn't say that he'd broken her heart. He had betrayed her every day without thinking twice about it, without even acknowledging that he'd done something wrong.

"You're too uptight," he'd told her when she confronted him about sleeping with his teaching assistant. "If you'd let me do what I want in our bed, I wouldn't have to go anywhere else."

For about half a second, she'd thought he might be right and that she needed to be more of a freak to satisfy her wandering man. Then she'd snapped out of it, slapped him hard across the face and told him to get the hell out of her condo. She'd cried, but they had been tears of self-pity, not heartbreak. After that experience, what did she want another man in her life for?

The box of condoms glinted at her from the gap in the bag. She quickly reached over and zipped it shut.

"Are you decent?" Seven called out from the other side of the door.

Bailey glared at the overnight bag with its hidden prophylactics. "The same as last time you saw me."

"In that case, I'll stay out here." Humor danced in his voice. "We're having an early dinner in about an hour and a half. Casual dress." He paused. "By the way, you don't have to endure my company if you don't want to. There are some books in the main room and plenty of channels on the idiot box."

He was awfully accommodating. Even under the circumstances, it was sweet. "Okay," she said. "I'll see you at dinner."

There was another pause then the slow sound of his footsteps fading away.

Seven was cooking dinner. Bailey walked into the dining room, fresh from a shower, to find him setting the table, with a kitchen towel over one shoulder, a Sam Cooke song on his lips. Cooking smells swirled around them. Fresh curry. Sage. Pepper. When he noticed her, he paused, the utensils halfway between his fingers and the table.

"You changed," he said.

"And showered."

He cleared his throat and went back to setting the table, glancing at her form in appreciation, a smile playing around his mouth before he turned away to go back to the adjoining galley. Bailey suddenly felt self-conscious in the dress she'd chosen to wear. It seemed the least ridiculous of her choices. It was a 1950s vintage dress, tight and white with red cherries all over it. She felt like a pinup girl.

"This is my sister's dress. You're right. She did make some interesting choices when she packed a weekend bag for me."

He didn't comment on the "weekend" part of her statement, probably recognizing that she was fishing for information about how long they'd be gone. During her shower, she'd made peace with the fact that she would miss work on Monday, maybe even Tuesday, and that the partners would be okay with it. Her sister was a very convincing liar.

Seven brought two covered platters to the table, then went back to the galley for a pitcher with something yellow in it. Lemonade?

"Bette has good taste. It's very different from what I've seen you wear, but I like it."

Bailey imagined him suddenly being interested in her sister. Bette, the more fun one. The one with fewer hangups in the bedroom and out of it. "Don't think you'll get an accommodating concubine during this trip," she snapped. "That's not going to happen." Then she bit the inside of her cheek. *Stop being so stupid, Bailey.*

He looked at her with mild reproach as he put two glasses next to their empty plates. "You have a lot of assumptions about what I do and don't want to do with you on this trip."

"What else do I have to go on? You haven't told me what we're doing." It drove her crazy to be in the dark about his plans, but she was trying to take her sister's advice and going with the flow. It wouldn't hurt. Right?

"Let's eat," Seven said.

She sat across from him at the table. Outside, the sun was still a bright burning disk in the sky. It felt strange to be eating dinner so early. Seven removed the cover from the platters and put them aside. Bailey gawked at what he'd made. What looked like curried chicken and white rice, and a pretty cabbage, carrot and corn medley. She'd never been with a man who could cook.

"The curry chicken might be a little spicy," he said. "But I think you can handle it."

"I love spicy food." She served herself some of everything, including the drink in the pitcher. She didn't miss the look of approval he gave her.

"That's pineapple juice," he said. "Fresh."

She tasted the juice, rolling the faintly tart sweetness around on her tongue. It was better than anything she'd ever gotten from the store.

"This is good," she said. "Thank you. I didn't expect you to make dinner and drinks for us."

"I like to keep you off balance," he said.

"You're doing a damn good job of it." She picked up her fork, considering his words.

It was one thing to miss out on two or three workdays. It was another to let go of every reservation she'd had about men, and about this man in particular. He was still off-limits. The idea of inviting someone like him into her life for anything long-term frightened her. But maybe Bette was right. There was nothing wrong with having fun as long as they were both clear on what was going on.

Bailey sank her fork into a piece of chicken with its sprinkling of thyme and pepper. The chicken parted under the tines with very little urging. In her mouth, it was tender and well seasoned. Familiar but like nothing else she'd ever had before.

With that first bite, she suddenly realized how hungry she was. She'd been too upset to eat much earlier that afternoon. Now she was starving. Bailey reached for another forkful, then another.

"This is the best Jamaican food I've ever had," she said, covering her mouth with one hand as she chewed. "Your mother taught you well." She eyed the platter in the middle of the table, wondering if it was bad manners to get seconds even though she was still working on her first.

Seven uncovered the food and scooped spoonfuls of everything onto Bailey's plate. She smiled at him in thanks.

"Actually, my father taught me to cook," he said. "He is the better cook of the two of them. Mama likes to bake."

With her fork, Bailey split a piece of potato, then put the larger piece in her mouth. "Does that mean you have a three-layer cake hidden somewhere around here?" That actually didn't sound too bad to her about now. But she was just being greedy.

"No, I'm not that ambitious." Seven drank from his glass of juice, watching her with a pleased smile. "I like challenges, but only those with at least a slim likelihood of success."

"Are you trying to tell me you can't bake? Because if so, you might as well turn this boat around right now." Bailey forked gravy-soaked rice into her mouth and nearly groaned aloud with appreciation. The rice was firm, the grains unbroken from the cooking process, just like she preferred. It soaked up the flavors of the curry perfectly, adding a buttery nuttiness of its own.

"Hopefully, I *succeeded* in telling you I can't bake. That's one expectation I won't be able to live up to. But—" Seven held up his fork "—I can guarantee you some good pastry at the end of our trip."

Pastry? *This man must want me to marry him.* Pastries were her longtime weakness. "What makes you think I have any expectations about you?"

"I'd be surprised if you didn't. You already think I have petty designs on your body. God knows what else you think I'm about."

She smiled, slowing down the pace of her eating as she became more full. "I told you, I don't have many."

"But you do have some. Tell me."

She laughed, unable to stop the heat under her cheeks. Damn Bette and her ridiculous conversation. She was definitely not going to let him know she and her sister had been speculating about the size of his...equipment.

"What? You think all Jamaican guys have big penises?"

She choked on her forkful of rice, coughed and could not answer him.

"That's it, isn't it?" Seven laughed with delight. His head fell back to reveal the strong column of his throat. "I'm flattered."

Bailey watched him, enjoying the sight of his uninhibited laughter. Tentatively, she let her bad side come out to play. "Is that a way for you to avoid the question?"

His laughter fell away and he looked at her across the table, lips twitching still in amusement. "Not at all."

"So tell me." She sipped on her pineapple juice, not taking her eyes off him.

"I don't think I'm any more or less endowed than any other Jamaican man I've seen."

"And how many Jamaican men have you seen naked?" She winced. This sounded like one of those questions women ask when considering a man as a dating prospect. Are you gay? Do you still live with your mother? What's the size of your penis?

Instead of being offended, he laughed again. "Probably all the men on both sides of the family at one time or another. We go to the seaside and down by the river fairly often. Sometimes it's a spontaneous trip and no one has swimsuits."

For a moment, Bailey was struck dumb by the sudden image of Seven and a bunch of men who looked like him running naked out into the sea. She cleared her throat. "Really?"

"Yeah, man. It's just the body. We all have one. When I'm at home, I don't wear many clothes anyhow." He shrugged.

Again, the image of Seven came to her, this time alone and in his kitchen, or what she imagined his kitchen to look like, towel thrown over a bare, muscular shoulder, the muscles in his butt flexing as he walked between the kitchen counter and stove with a platter of freshly made jerk chicken. A beautiful fantasy.

"Are you picturing me naked now?" He raised a playful eyebrow.

"Yes, actually."

"And?"

"It's difficult for me to imagine what an average Jamaican man looks like. There."

"Do you want me to show you?"

Bailey had known that question was coming the minute the last word left her mouth, but she still wasn't prepared for it. Her mouth dried. *Time to put up or shut up,* she thought.

"Yes, I would."

Seven's eyebrow arched again and, for a moment, she thought she'd won. Then he put down his fork, stood up from the table and reached for his fly.

Bailey opened her mouth to give in. To tell him never mind. But nothing came out. Seven flicked open the button of his shorts. The sound of the zipper split the air. He wore black briefs. Bailey processed the information about his underwear, the thickness of him pressing against the dark cotton, before she turned her head away and closed her eyes.

If they did this now, she felt things would change irrevocably between them. She knew it was just looking, but it felt so significant in a way she could not ignore. Some days she wanted to be like Bette and play as if life had no consequences, but she couldn't. Not with Seven.

"Okay, you win!" She kept her eyes closed.

"This is not a game, Bailey," he said. "If you want to see me, I'll show you. I have nothing to hide."

Things had become too serious.

"No." She gestured at his fly without turning around. "I'm not ready for that." Her voice was high with panic.

"It wouldn't mean anything," Seven said.

Bailey opened her eyes but still did not turn around. "It would mean something."

She heard the sound of Seven's zipper going back up, the chair creak with his weight, the fork clicking against the side of the plate as he picked it up and resumed his dinner. Bailey turned around to see him looking gravely at her.

"I would have stopped it there, you know," he said.

"I know, but maybe I wouldn't have." The truth of it resounded in the room, her desire for him bare at last, the possibility between them bursting into bloom. She licked her lips and reached for the glass of juice. It was empty. Before she could pick up the pitcher, he was pouring some into her cup.

"So, I guess you've never played Show Me Yours and I'll Show You Mine?" he asked, his mouth tilting up in a faint smile.

Despite getting what he wanted—her to admit that she wanted him—he was a graceful winner. Bailey smiled.

"No. I don't like games."

"Not even when you were a little child? The innocent games are fun, too. Naming all the things that begin with the letter *L* that you see. Although, that one was mainly for road trips."

"I played with Bette when I was little, I just don't remember the games." She went back to her meal, somber now.

"How about hide-and-seek?"

She laughed. "That one, I remember."

"Oh, good. Pop quiz later."

"Boy, please." Bailey waved her hand dismissively and smiled.

From there, their teasing banter emerged even more under his careful tending. He refilled her glass when it needed refilling, and when she was done eating that tremendous amount of food, he took her empty plate away to the sink. The sound of the boat moving quickly over the water was white noise, ignorable, immaterial, as the juice was finished and Seven refilled her glass with water. They moved from the dining table to the kitchen, where they washed dishes together, then to the salon. Bailey collapsed on the leather sofa, such a luxurious caress against her skin to accompany the sweet lassitude moving through her body from her overfull belly.

"If you've brought me here to fatten me up for the kill, you've succeeded," she murmured.

Bailey could feel her eyes falling shut, her body curling into itself, the sun falling on her legs through the windows. Seven said something, but she barely heard him. He draped a thin sheet over her. She muttered his name and reached for him, knowing what she wanted but not able to articulate it. Her body was heavy, so heavy.

Seven murmured something else, a denial maybe, and Bailey pulled him harder down to her. Then somehow, he was on the couch, under her, his scent snuggled close, and his breathing deep and even beneath her ear. She fell asleep.

Chapter 14

She was on top of him. Incredibly. Impossibly. It was as if she'd drunk a bottle of whiskey and passed out. Seven had never seen anything like it. The way she had devoured his food as if she'd never had anything as good in her life. Even in the midst of questioning him, of teasing him, she had eaten. It was the sexiest thing he'd ever seen in his life.

And after they'd eaten, she'd begun to relax. They'd talked about childhood games, about games they'd played or wanted to play as adults.

"I don't play games," she'd said.

But he had seen the longing in her eyes for something more playful. Maybe she didn't know how to get in touch with that part of herself, but it was definitely something that she wanted. Another chance at a childhood she thought she'd missed out on.

"My parents were always playing games. My sister, too. I had to be the stable one in the family, always."

As they'd talked, she'd slowly sunk into the couch, her words becoming softer and softer. The thread of coherence had loosened until she'd stopped talking altogether and only breathed softly on the couch, her lips slightly parted in sleep.

When he'd come over with a blanket to cover her, she'd

opened her eyes and reached for him, said his name in an achingly sweet way he would never forget.

"I think you drugged me," she'd said.

"I wouldn't do that to you."

"But you would kidnap me." Her words had been sluggish.

"Yes, and I'd do it again."

She'd made a soft noise, tired of talking; then a surprisingly strong hand had clutched his arm.

"Come here."

He'd come and she'd tried to make him get onto the couch next to her, which hadn't quite worked, since the couch was meant for only one to sleep on. So he'd arranged them both, with her on top of him, her head tucked under his chin. She'd slept.

He couldn't sleep. It seemed strange, strangely good, that at her most vulnerable, she wanted him there with her. He was aware of her slight weight on him, the cocoa butter smell of her skin, her legs tangled with his. She was a minor miracle in his arms, the way she abandoned herself completely to sleep in his presence. Everything seemed backward. Weren't they supposed to get to this part after making love, after...everything?

His father had always told him his expectations would be the ruin of him.

"Be open to surprises," Winston Carmichael had said to him and his brother more than once. "When things don't go according to your plan, that doesn't mean there isn't a larger one at work that will make things work out the way they should."

With a deep breath, Seven deliberately released his expectations. His father was right. This woman was here with him now, and that was all that mattered. Already, she had softened to him since the start of their boat ride. A woman of surprises.

Gradually he relaxed. He gently caressed her back and settled into the couch. Soon, he slept.

He woke slowly. Aware of his surroundings, the scud of the boat on the water, sunlight and blue sky through the oversize windows of the yacht, and the woman sleeping in his arms. Although he'd never been one to keep religion, as his father did, he felt blessed. He breathed deeply of those blessings and felt Bailey stir in his arms. She made a soft noise and snuggled deeper into chest. Then she froze. Slowly, she lifted her head and met his eyes.

Seven grinned. "I didn't peek while you were asleep, I promise."

Confusion clouded her eyes for a moment before they cleared. "How long have I been asleep?" She covered her mouth with her hand and slowly pushed her body up and away from him.

"No more than an hour, I'm assuming. It's still daylight." Although the sky was darkening toward sunset. "But we should get ready. We're about to stop."

She pulled the dress down over her thighs, ran fingers through her hair and stood up. "Where are we going?"

"You'll see," he said.

"Is this another game of yours?"

"Maybe."

She shook her head. "I'm going to brush my teeth and do something about this hair. Then I'll be ready for whatever craziness you have planned." Bailey walked toward the hallway and the suite of rooms. Unrepentantly, Seven watched the sway of her little behind in the dress. Her feet were bare.

He shook himself and stood up, looked at his watch. Yes,

definitely time to get ready. He blew hot breath into his palm. And definitely time for him to brush his teeth, too.

Nearly fifteen minutes later, he knocked on her door.

"Yes?"

"Finish up your beauty regimen or the boat leaves without you."

"We're already on a boat."

"Good point."

The sound of her laughter came from behind the door. "I'll be ready in ten minutes."

"Meet me up on deck and wear sensible shoes."

"My shoes are always sensible," he heard her call out as he walked away.

True to her word, she was ready a little less than ten minutes later. She emerged from belowdecks, wearing the same heart-stopping dress as before, but instead of those skyscraper heels of hers, she wore flat sandals. A tiny white purse was attached to her wrist by an even smaller strap.

Her hair was an asymmetrical cascade of curls over her head, a few falling into her face and across one eye. "I'm ready."

"Have you been here before?"

For the first time, she seemed to be aware of where they were, that the boat was docked near about half a dozen others. With the sun diving toward sunset, people wound lazily around the dock but seemed headed for a common destination. He took her hand and led her off the boat.

"Where is here?"

That answered his question rightly enough. "Key West."

From nearby came the sound of drums and many voices, a celebration. They walked under an archway with the proclamation Welcome to Mallory Square.

"Oh." She looked around as he guided her with a touch

at the small of her back through the growing crowd. "Bette comes down here all the time."

"She's here all the time but you never come?" He put it in the form of a question, knowing what her answer would be.

"I work a lot. I'm not able to get away."

"That's bull and you know it. The trip is so short, how can you not have time to make it down?"

She gave him a look and wrinkled her nose. "Remember, I told you I wasn't fun."

"Everyone's fun," he said. "Especially when they're with me." He waggled his eyebrows, gave her a glimpse of his excellent teeth.

She laughed. A rowdy group of teens pushed through the crowd, bumping into the tall man wearing dreadlocks who walked near them. Seven pulled her against him to keep the same thing from happening to her. When the kids moved on, laughing and jumping on each other's backs, she didn't move away from him.

"I don't live the life of leisure that you and my sister do," she said after a moment.

"But you do live." He gently squeezed her waist. Before she could say anything else, he spun her toward him and pulled her belly against his, smiling. People in the crowd made room for them, a few giving looks of approval, and envy. Who wouldn't envy him the company of this gorgeous woman? The wind blew back Bailey's curls and she met his smile with one of her own. "Just hush and let me show you what's in your own backyard."

Her arms fell around his waist. "Okay. Just this once." Her eyes glimmered.

They resumed their walk, and she kept a hand around his waist, watching the crowd with the intense curiosity of a child. Street performers were scattered all around them. Up ahead, a brown-skinned woman in a simple white dress played the violin, a haunting classical piece, while pass-ersby dropped money into her open violin case. A few chil-dren and their parents stood around her to watch and listen.

Marcus had told Seven about the sunset celebration at Mallory Square in Key West days before, when Seven's wealthy friend had been wondering how to next occupy his seemingly endless stretch of free time. His girls, two new ones plus the blonde whose name he couldn't remem-ber, had shown up at Seven's condo out of sheer boredom.

"There's only so much shopping and screwing you can do," Marcus had said with a whine.

Seven couldn't sympathize. But when Marcus had men-tioned the sunset celebration as a place to take the boat for a drive, it had seemed perfect for Bailey.

He and Bailey walked through the heavy weekend crowd on the square, passing the vendors with their scarves, hand-made photo frames, jewelry and nearly everything else under the sun for sale. At his side, Bailey watched it all with a look that grew more and more distant.

They passed a woman with silver jewelry on display and Bailey stopped to look. There was nothing there that Seven thought she'd ever wear, but she talked to the woman for a long while, even bought one of her big turquoise rings. After walking in silence, drinking in the air of celebration and vibrancy, Bailey looked up at him.

"I grew up with people like this," she said. "My parents called themselves 'serious artists,' but they loved being around hippies and people who walked on fire. All this." She gestured to the madness around them.

Seven kept his arm around her waist, pleased that she was talking about her past with him.

"Do you see your parents often?" he asked.

"They're dead."

Seven smoothed her waist. "I'm sorry to hear that. It must be hard not having them around anymore."

"It's actually easier," she said.

She shrugged off his hand and walked quickly ahead, weaving through the crowd, a melancholy beauty in her cherry-and-white dress. She stopped at a street dancer, watching the brown boy contort his body to music from a nearby boom box.

Bailey reached into the small purse attached to her wrist for five dollars and dropped it into the dancer's white bucket. Seven caught up to her. Watched the thin boy, who seemed no more than a teenager, do handstands and jerk his body to some drum-and-bass music. The audience applauded as he did a flip and landed firmly on his feet.

"You can't really believe it's easier for them to be dead," he said as they moved away from the dancer.

A chorus of alarmed gasps rose up ahead where an acrobat was performing. A couple near them quickened their steps toward the gasps just as the crowd broke out in congratulatory and relieved applause. Scattered among the artists were tattooed pirates, children with painted faces, hippies in tie-dyed skirts, even a dog dressed in shorts.

But Bailey wasn't happy at all. Maybe bringing her here had been a mistake. Among this vibrant art and beauty she only saw bad reminders of her childhood.

She looked at him over her shoulder, her face closed off. "I don't want to talk about them anymore."

He nodded. But as the evening wore on, it was obvious she was still thinking about them. He managed to tease her out of her initial funk, buying a tiny stuffed dog wearing Hawaiian shorts, and presenting it to her as a peacemaking gift. As was getting to be her habit with him, she shook her head but couldn't hide her smile.

"You are a fool," she said.

"Only for you."

Her smile lingered as they made their way through the festive crowd, but it was obvious she was still thinking about her parents.

Suddenly, she gasped. "Oh, my God, he's going to kill himself!"

She gripped his hand as they watched the tattooed and ponytailed acrobat balance on a dirty rope above a forty-foot drop into the water below. But the middle-aged man backflipped perfectly and retained his perch on the rope. The crowd applauded and Bailey did, too, taking Seven's hand again after raining her claps and a few dollar bills on the man. Seven thought about teasing her for holding his hand, but he knew that would only make her pull away. He tightened his fingers around hers.

"Come on, I can't watch anymore." Bailey tugged him away from the acrobat, toward a skinny bare-chested young man juggling flaming batons while riding a ten-foot-tall unicycle. The boy flirted with the crowd as he tossed his flames in the air, smiling at one woman or another all the while.

"This is less dangerous?" He laughed.

"Yes, of course. That's nothing. My uncle Max used to do this all the time. He—" Suddenly, she stopped, the lights in her eyes fading to nothing. She bit her lip, tossed her hair away from her face. "Never mind. It's not important."

They stayed to watch the boy finish his act.

"You may not be impressed by that boy," Seven said as they left the young man to start his act again for a new crowd, "but I never had an Uncle Max. The closest thing I had to that was Auntie Terri, who could climb a coconut tree and drop down three or four coconuts with her machete in one minute flat." He looked down at Bailey. "I never knew how she could do all that in a dress and high heels."

Send For
2 FREE BOOKS
Today!

I accept your offer!

Please send me two
free novels and two mystery
gifts (gifts worth about $10).
I understand that these books
are completely free—even
the shipping and handling will
be paid—and I am under no
obligation to purchase anything,
ever, as explained on the back
of this card.

168/368 XDL F429

Please Print

FIRST NAME

LAST NAME

ADDRESS

APT.#   CITY

STATE/PROV.   ZIP/POSTAL CODE

Visit us online at
www.ReaderService.com

She giggled and dipped her forehead against his shoulder. The night rang with joyous voices. A small dog barking for attention. Scattered applause rang out along the pier. Here and there shoppers haggled with vendors over the prices of their goods. Bailey's hand slid from his. She moved even closer to him to wrap her arm around his waist.

"It's magical here," she said. "Thank you for bringing me."

"I'm glad you're enjoying it. For a minute there, I was worried. I still am, actually."

"Don't be worried." She smiled that sad smile of hers again. "Bette was right. I do need this."

They strolled in silence among the stalls, Bailey touching a miniature painting of the sunset, a small blown-glass bird, one of over a dozen baskets made from palm fronds. But she bought nothing else.

They wandered away from the crowd, neither of them speaking, the foot traffic getting more and more sparse until they left the madness of Mallory Square and the pier completely behind, walking through roads fringed by palm trees and quaint two-story buildings that glowed under the street lamps. From nearby, the sound of a woman's laughter rose up into the night.

"You know, art was everything to my parents," Bailey finally said. "They surrounded themselves with it, they created it, everywhere the family moved was because Daddy or Mama got some sort of fellowship or residency." She stopped in the middle of the street to look up at Seven. Under the streetlights, her gaze was haunted and young. "When they died, I swore I wouldn't be like them."

Seven touched her face. "But you are like them," he said gently. "Your work is your life. You don't make room for anything else."

She bit her lip and dropped her gaze to somewhere beyond his shoulder. He was immediately sorry for what he'd said. It was the truth, but maybe she wasn't ready to hear it. Seven looked around the quiet street where they stood, at the for-sale sign in the yard, with the big red-and-white sign above it that said Pool.

"Forget what I said." He grabbed her hand. It was his turn to lead. "Come on."

Chapter 15

"Where are we going?"

"You ask too many questions." Seven laughed as he pulled her along onto the manicured lawn of a house that was obviously empty.

The wide-open windows and mint-green exterior made the house seem homey even as they flew past, with Seven towing her along. They went to the back of the house, where a six-foot-tall fence stopped them.

"Nice try," he muttered to himself, then let go of Bailey's hand to hop over the tall wooden fence. A moment later, the gate unlatched and Seven appeared, smiling. "Come."

Bailey shook her head. This was not a good idea. She glanced nervously around, sure that someone was peering out at them and was about to call the police.

"What the hell are you doing?" She dropped her voice to a whisper. "This is trespassing. We're going to get shot."

He tugged her inside the gate and clicked it shut. Behind the gate, the house was even more beautiful. Tall windows allowed a view into a more-than-modest conch-style two-story. The house was completely bare, as far as Bailey could see. Not a piece of furniture in sight. An old-fashioned street lamp illuminated the backyard, which was well tended, with low carpet grass, a water fountain and the swimming pool.

Seven stood at the edge of the pool, clean except for a few floating leaves from the nearby mango tree.

"Let's not waste this," he said and pulled off his shirt.

"What are you doing?"

"What does it look like?" He unbuttoned and unzipped his shorts and pulled them down his muscular thighs before Bailey could say anything else.

Her mouth dropped open and she stared. *Damn, he's beautiful.* Then he pulled off his briefs and threw them on top of his other clothes. Bailey swallowed.

"Come in with me."

She shook her head. "No. The cops could come by any second."

"Only if you keep talking so loud."

She lowered her voice. "I don't want to do this."

He shrugged. "Fine, then don't." And he dove into the water with a gentle splash.

Bailey blinked, holding on to the image of his incredible body, tight and muscled, brown and beautiful all over. Her first impression of him was completely on target. He was perfect.

Seven swam in the water, graceful as an eel, completely at home in a stranger's pool.

"The water's warm," he said, rising up from the surface near her.

The water sluiced down his face, spiking his lashes, running down his full lips and down to his wide chest. Then he pushed back from the wall to float on his back.

Lord, have mercy. Bailey wiped her suddenly damp palms on the back of her dress. He looked like all her fantasies come to life, every single lip-biting one of them.

Girl, if you don't get on top of that man... She could hear her sister's voice plainly in the back of her mind, like the devil urging her on. He was beautiful beyond a doubt, but she had never been one for casual sex, and this thing with him was doomed for failure. If she slept with him she might as well just declare her heart broken and get it over with.

But you don't have to sleep with him. Just go for a swim. Just a swim. Right.

"This is the life right here." Seven groaned softly from the water. He dove down to the deep end of the pool, then came back up, face serious, eyes smiling. "Have you ever wondered what a life truly lived feels like?" he asked.

Forget you, Bailey thought. Without giving herself time to think about it, she took off her dress and panties and dove into the water. It *was* warm! The water caressed every inch of her bare skin in a way that she'd never experienced before as a virgin to skinny-dipping. Seven laughed, as delighted as a schoolboy, when she surfaced next to him, shoving her limp hair out of her eyes.

"Screw you," she said to him, swimming closer.

He laughed again. "I'm ready whenever you are."

Bailey had come closer with the intent to threaten—and to prove to Seven that she was not afraid of her life, that she could do whatever she wanted. But closer to him was more dangerous. His skin radiated warmth as he treaded water in the deep end, sending out ripples from his movements.

"Stop that," she said.

"What?"

"You know what." She blinked water from her eyes. "You know this can't work, but you're still trying to force it. Square pegs don't fit into round holes, Seven."

"I know what fits into round holes, Bailey." His voice was low, deep. Seductive.

Bailey swallowed. And still came closer.

"You're not playing fair."

"I want you. There is no fair in this."

She kissed him.

He drew her into him, completing the move she'd made by claiming her mouth, kissing her deeply as if he'd wanted her for hours, days, weeks. Bailey clung to his strength, allowed the hot hardness of his tongue in her mouth, the unyielding surface of his chest under her breasts, the heat rising up from her center to meet his. *This is good.*

She wrapped her legs around him in the water, felt him work to keep them both afloat, then, groaning, give up, moving backward until the edge of the pool was at his back. Cement grazed Bailey's knees. Still she pressed closer to him, the fire of his body scalding her from the outside in.

His hardness pressed against her and she pressed back. She clasped her palms against his cheeks, drinking from his lips, wanting more and more and more.

He pulled away from her, gasping. "If we don't stop now, I—" He swallowed heavily, his Adam's apple bobbing in his throat. "I don't have anything with me to protect you, Bailey."

She panted, clinging to him, her hands still flat against his cheeks as if she meant to devour him. His hardness pushed even more insistently against her center despite his words. Bailey dropped her legs from around him, blinking away the haze of passion. How could he be so logical at a time like this? After all, he'd started this. He'd… Bailey forced herself to take a deep breath. She touched his neck, shoulders, breathed in his particular woodsy scent, which she suddenly realized was not just his cologne. She swallowed and forced her body into some semblance of calm. *But he feels so good!*

"I thought you said you were an average-sized Jamaican man."

"I am," he said, pushing his hips once more into hers so she felt again the weight and size of him.

Mercy. Bailey allowed herself the luxury of his touch,

the heat of his skin through the water, the memory of his taste on her tongue. Then she took another deep breath and pushed herself away from him, did a graceful turn under the water, soaking her head to get him out of it, then swam for the edge of the pool. She pulled herself out and went for her clothes.

"Let's go back to the boat," she said.

Bailey walked away from him and did not look back.

They made it back to the boat, wrapped in the silence of their separate thoughts. Once on board, the crew didn't waste any time pulling them out of the port and continuing on their journey. Bailey went to her room.

As soon as she walked in, she noticed her overnight bag on the trunk at the foot of the bed. She remembered the condoms in her bag, then cursed herself for the memory. Sleeping with him would be a bad idea.

But it would feel so good.

What if he was terrible in bed? Then that would be one way to get over him. If he was bad in bed, then all her questions were answered. She could let go of her little ill-advised obsession with him and get back to her normal life. And then what?

It had been a long time since she'd been with a man. Not since Clive, and that was an embarrassingly long time ago. After him, she couldn't trust anyone else, didn't want anyone else. She'd determined that what she wanted was a man who fit her criteria. She'd been so careful to avoid all the wrong men and not repeat her mistakes.

Clive had been handsome, charming, an intellectual who didn't talk down to people and who wanted kids of his own. But on the night of her first date, she'd noticed him watching the waitress with a very avaricious look. Later, as she'd walked back from the bathroom, she thought she saw Clive chatting up that same waitress and exchanging numbers with her. But she'd brushed that off as impossible. Why would a man do something like that?

She shouldn't have gone out with him on another date, or agreed to be his girlfriend, and she should definitely not have agreed to marry him. At times, she'd wondered if infidelity wasn't just something every man did. Women had children. Men had multiple women. Still, that wasn't something she wanted to compromise on.

Enter Seven, the perfect man in nearly every way. Except the most important way. His irresponsibility had led them to go swimming naked in a stranger's pool, for heaven's sake. What if the police had come and arrested them? What if the owners had happened by? Then all Bailey had built in her safe and sane world would have come tumbling down. She didn't want that. She didn't want any insecurity.

But if she didn't want any of that, then why was her mouth still tingling from his kisses? Why was her body throbbing to complete what they'd started in that pool? The obvious answer was that he was sexy as hell. Knees weak and falling-backward-on-the-bed kind of sexy.

She looked over her shoulder at her overnight bag again.

A knock sounded at the door, and although she knew who it was, she jumped. What did he want? Hopefully not to finish what they'd started in that stranger's backyard. Despite knowing better, a steady and hard pulse began to beat between her thighs at the thought.

"Get a grip!" she growled to herself.

"Did you say something?" Seven asked from the other side of the door.

"No. Just a second." She looked into the mirror and winced at her limp and fuzzy hair. But he'd seen her like that for the entire walk back to the boat. Still, she smoothed it as best she could, tugged the hem of her dress down her thighs and opened the door.

"Hey," she greeted him brightly.

"Hey." His gaze swept her from head to foot, seemed to miss nothing.

The pulse inside Bailey beat harder.

"I came to apologize," he said. "I shouldn't have done what I did. I'm taking us back home."

She stared at him. "After all that, you're just going to take us home?" The words fell from her mouth in a rush, surprising her.

"Yes," Seven said. "Isn't that what you want?"

"This is supposed to be my vacation, isn't that what you said? Things may not go exactly the way you planned, but that's no reason we can't finish what you started."

He stood in the doorway, shaking his head. "Once again, you surprise me," he said.

She smiled, stepping close to him. "If you'd wanted a predicable woman you wouldn't be chasing me, now, would you?"

A slow smile unfurled from his lips. "You're very right about that."

Bailey finally had to admit to herself that she liked this man. She enjoyed his company, his smile, and she sure as hell liked flirting with him, even though it was a bad idea.

"Keep the boat on course, Seven. I'll be here for the ride until the end."

His smile drifted away. "Keep talking like that and you'll give a man the wrong ideas, Ms. Hughes."

She shook her head. "I already told you how this has to be."

"Yes, you did." His voice was heavy with regret.

She pressed her hand against his chest and pushed. "Go

mope somewhere else. I'm going to read for a while then go to bed."

"All right," he said. "Good night." He hesitated for a moment, then bent his head to kiss her briefly on the mouth. "See you tomorrow."

His lips brushed hers with a light tenderness. As he pulled away, she curled her hand into his shirt, held him close. His and her lips. He made a low noise of surprise as she deepened the kiss, pressing her mouth to his.

What are you doing?

But whatever logic that had been ruling her minutes before fled with the touch of his mouth on hers. The chlorine and sweat scent of him, the insistent pulse beat between her thighs. Bailey whimpered softly in surrender, slipping her arms up and around his neck.

There was no hesitation in Seven. His arms claimed her waist, drew her closer. Kissed her until her head was spinning with the force of her desire, and her pulse became a pounding drumbeat between her thighs. She shoved her hands up under his T-shirt, palms over his belly and chest, tracing the thick muscle and sleek flesh.

This was what she wanted. This and this and this.

The passion rose up between them quickly, pulling them under as if they'd never left the pool. Bailey raked her fingers over his stiff little nipples, sucked his tongue into her mouth, while a river of lust flowed between her legs. She felt Seven's hands on her bottom, pulling her hard against his body, against his rigid sex, squeezing her through the dress.

He groaned and crushed her against him. His mouth on hers. Her arms wrapped around his waist. Her hips pressed to his. He was even harder against her belly, the insistent brand of his desire feeding hers. Firm tongue. His hot mouth. Seven's hands tugged off her dress, the underwear.

Bailey clawed off his shirt, fingers frantic on the closure of his shorts, the elastic band of underwear, until they were naked together, breaths coming quickly, tongues twining, mouths sliding together, Bailey's needful noises rising up around them. The smell of her arousal shocked her with its potency. Made her want him even more.

She whispered his name. He made a tortured sound, then released her. Pulled his mouth from hers. She whimpered in protest, clung to him. Licked his chest, his nipples, bit them.

"Shit!" He groaned and flung his head back. "I have to go get some—" He gestured to his sex.

The fog of desire lifted just enough for Bailey to understand what he was talking about. She dumped out the contents of the bag her sister had left her, grabbed a condom. Her hand shook as she gave it to Seven. He made a harsh sound of relief, ripped the foil packet open.

He rolled on the rubber, lifted her up, groaning against her mouth. Her legs slipped around his waist, her sex opening up against his, the parted lips of her desire sliding against his hard length. She squirmed against him. Then her back was to the wall. And he was inside her. Full. Hard. Strong.

She threw her head back and groaned out a curse of pleasure. "Fu…"

It was as if they were trapped in the vortex of desire from the night before, when Bailey would have done anything to feel him inside her. Her skin clawed for satisfaction. Seven gripped her flanks, filling her deeply. She felt every inch of him inside her, stroking her with his thickness. She gripped her legs even tighter around him and held on as he filled her with his desire and need. Her eyes fluttered shut.

His hand jerked in her hair. "No. Look at me."

The breath hiccuped in her throat when she opened her eyes and stared into his. Seven's eyes were molten with desire for her. Burning. Bailey gasped. She trembled as he pinned her to the wall with his powerful body, his hardness moving deeply, firmly inside her.

He let go of her hair and touched her breasts, tugging on her nipples until they were painfully hard, until she groaned from it, until her sex was drowning in its own wetness. They moved slowly together, hips snaking, breaths panting as the pleasure stretched between them like taffy, hot and sticky. Seven oozed it, dripped with it as he took her, his fullness almost more than she could bear. Their eyes held. He moved inside her. She panted. Sank her fingers into his arms, which slid beneath hers with sweat.

She wanted him to move faster. He knew she wanted him to move faster. But he held her firmly to the wall, his thrusts slow and heavy, ramming so deeply into her, so sweetly she thought she would scream from the pleasure of it. Her body burned from the sweet fire. But she wanted more. She *needed* more. After lusting after Seven for what felt like an eternity, she simply wanted it hot and fast and fierce and now.

Seven's hand gripped her hips as he took her, controlling the pace of their coming together. Bailey was done with that. It felt as though she had waited so long for him. For this moment. She wanted everything now. The force of his orgasm, uncontrolled. Now. Inside her. Bailey locked her legs around him and rolled her hips, moved faster around him, pumping her hips in counterpoint to his. Fast. Faster. Seven swallowed hard, the pulse thudding like a drum in his throat.

"No!" He gasped, sweat dripping down his face. Body like a furnace against hers.

"Yes."

She sank her nails even deeper into his flesh until he cried out, gasping as she moved quickly on him, gripping him, speeding toward the conclusion they both wanted. Then it was his lashes that fluttered, his body falling mercy to her desires as her sex gripped him, dragged around him, squeezed and released him. Milked him. He lost himself inside her, crying out just as she found her release, riding the last of his strength until her satisfaction spilled over them both.

Seven buried his face in her throat, his hand somehow caught in her hair again. His breath was hot and fast against her skin.

"Damn. I wanted to take this slowly."

"But I didn't," she panted.

She tightened her sex around him and he bucked against her, pulled out, pulled away, forcing Bailey to loosen her legs around him. Her head fell back against the wall as her breath slowed. She licked her lips. Closed her eyes. Savoring the tiny orgasmic twitches still moving through her body. The slight soreness she could already feel from the size of him.

Seven chuckled softly. "I like a woman who knows what she wants."

He lifted her into his arms and she gasped at the suddenness of it. Then they were on the bed and pressed together, kissing and touching each other, Seven's hand between her legs, stroking her wetness, one finger, then two inside her, loving her. His mouth on her breasts. His tongue licking her nipples, pulling sounds of pleasure from her mouth. This time, she let him take his time, tugging the orgasm from between her legs one slow thrust at a time until she was panting his name and exploding into a thousand pieces underneath him.

Bailey's body wilted in the aftermath of her pleasure. She was limp against the sheets, swimming in the warm glow of satisfied lust when sleep found her and pulled her down.

* * *

When she woke up the next morning, he was gone. The sheets whispered under her as she rolled over, tugging a pillow against her face. She inhaled the faint scent of Seven that lingered on the pillowcase, remembering how his body had felt inside hers, the pleasure of it. And she questioned what that pleasure meant, if anything. She had wanted him so badly last night that nothing else had mattered. Now, with daylight and sanity returning, she wondered if she hadn't made a big mistake.

He had kidnapped her.

Getting her into bed had been his goal all along.

She had fallen right into his trap.

Bailey shoved the pillow away and stared up at the ceiling. Soon enough, she got tired of her mental meandering and got up, showered and went up on deck to find Seven. He wasn't anywhere she could see, although by the time it occurred to her to look in the pilothouse, she felt ridiculous for trying to find him. She stood on deck in shorts and a tank top, the wind whipping through her hair and tugging at her clothes.

She wondered if he regretted what had happened between them. Or was he crowing in triumph to the other men on the boat? Or, after chasing her so relentlessly, had her aggressiveness turned him off?

Bailey made a sound of frustration. Morning-after second-guessing. Another reason she hated dating. She shoved her hands in her shorts pockets, deliberately turning her mind away from Seven. She blinked out at the ocean.

The water was so blue it hurt. A gorgeous day on the open sea with a fresh breeze and only a few other boats on the open water. A fishing boat passed by with a couple on board. They waved and Bailey waved back. As if she was on vacation.

Her mother had loved the sea. Once, Maxine Hughes had borrowed a friend's small rowboat and taken her two girls with her. She'd sat in that small boat with a big floppy white hat on her head, rowing onto blue water. Rowing and rowing without a destination. Bailey and Bette were probably around five and six, content to play with the bucket of rocks and sponges their mother had carried along for them.

Bailey blinked at the sudden memory. Hot tears plucked at the backs of her eyes. She squeezed them shut, stood still, breathing in the whipping sea air until the urge to cry went away.

What's wrong with me?

She took a deep breath. This was all Seven's fault. If he hadn't brought her out here, then she wouldn't be dealing with this. She looked out to sea.

At the sunset celebration, she'd been assaulted by so many memories. Things she'd thought she'd forgotten about or forgiven. But as she walked through the collection of artists, madmen and hippies, everything about her childhood had come rushing back. Her parents taking them to art gallery and museum openings to gawk at the art and eat free food. Speeding through Venetian streets on the back of a motorcycle at night, her mother holding on to her for dear life, while up ahead, Bette rode an identically ancient bike while their father held on to her. Their parents had trusted them with so much. And they had been children. But— and she remembered her sister's words—they'd had fun. They'd experienced and done more by the age of sixteen than most people had by thirty. For better or worse, that had been life with her parents.

Bailey raked her hand through her hair, feeling the tears start again. She blew out a calming breath and walked away from the railing, determined not to dwell on her past for the rest of the day.

And she was successful, wandering the ship like a wraith. After failing to find Seven the first time, she'd simply avoided him and any potential of discussing the night they'd spent together, raiding the fridge in the galley when she got hungry, reading one of the paperbacks she'd found on the salon's bookshelf. Once she found that rhythm of aloneness, she actually enjoyed herself. Reading and eating alone, enjoying the fact of Seven's presence, the presence of the other two men on the boat, but feeling no pressure to see or talk to them. She didn't know how much time passed. She slept, woke, ate, read and slept again. Then, while she was belowdecks, stretched out in a strip of sunlight, the boat stopped.

Seven came to find her.

"Okay, lazybones." He dropped down to sit beside her. Seven touched her casually, making no indication that they'd shared a night of passion together. Bailey decided to play along. "We're here," he said.

She yawned and put her book facedown on the couch near her hip. "Where is here?"

"Come up and see."

Bailey yawned again and stood up with the aid of a strong pull from Seven's hand.

Outside the windows of the boat was nothing but the usual blue sky, although she could tell they had docked. The boat's purposeful flight from Miami was at an end. She allowed him to tug her by the gentle leash of his hand through the cool rooms of the boat and upstairs to the deck. As they emerged from below, a soft breeze caressed Bailey's face. Sweet. There was no other word for it. The air smelled sweet.

The *Dirty Diana* had found a temporary home in a small private dock. Already, the two crewmen stood on the dock in their white uniforms, stretching the kinks from their bodies. Beyond the boat, clear turquoise water stretched as far as Bailey looked. A couple of rowboats, faded blue from the sun and salt air, bobbed in the water near the blinding white sand that stretched peacefully bare for miles in both directions. Past the sand, dense foliage rose up around a footpath through the bushes.

Suddenly, she heard voices. Two men emerged from the footpath, both bare-chested. One was young, heavily bearded and wearing prescription glasses. The other older, clean-shaven and carrying a machete. Both handsome, with sun-darkened skin and a loose, relaxed way of walking.

"Bwoy, yu tek long time fi reach," the younger man called out from the sand.

Seven grinned. "We came as soon as we could."

He hurried Bailey off the boat with him. He hugged both men and clapped them on the back among a flurry of exchanged words that Bailey didn't understand. She looked around herself. Then looked at the men, who looked like Seven, even walked like him.

"It's good to see you, son." The older man embraced Seven with tender and special care.

"It's good to be seen, Papa."

Papa? Bailey looked around with dawning realization. They weren't in the United States anymore. They were in Jamaica.

Chapter 16

"We're in another country?"

She asked the question, incredulous, even though it was obvious where they were. She'd seen the postcards. They definitely weren't in Key West anymore. "I know, I know," she said when Seven opened his mouth to answer. "But how? We need passports, customs clearance."

"I took care of all that while you were asleep. Come." Seven swept her forward. "Meet my father and brother."

She suddenly felt self-conscious, too argumentative, too rumpled and casual to meet anyone new after days at sea.

"Winston Carmichael, Simon Carmichael. This is Bailey Hughes. A new friend from America."

"Friend, eh?" The older man chuckled then reached across his son to pull Bailey in for a hug. "Welcome to the island, girl."

His brother was not so easy. "You have to do better than that, brother." He looked her over with frank masculine interest, which seemed especially primal with his thick beard growing without any sort of shape or definition. "If she's just your friend, then that means she can make new friends here." Simon looked over his shoulder at his brother with a grin. "You look tired after your long travel, empress. Come rest yourself."

Bailey shook her head. If she still looked tired after all

those naps she'd taken on the boat, there was something seriously wrong with her. But she allowed Simon to usher her toward the path through the bushes.

"Don't spin her head with your foolishness, man!" Seven called out from the pier.

Bailey looked over her shoulder and saw him talking with the yacht's crew. She stopped. "No offence, gentlemen, but I'm not going anywhere without him."

"So he's your man, then?" Simon's eyes danced behind his round glasses.

Somehow she thought he knew about her situation with Seven and was just playing with her. "It wouldn't be polite for me to leave him, when he's the one who brought me here."

"Leave Seven's woman alone." The older man playfully slapped his son on the leg with the flat side of his machete. "You have your own piece of business to take care of here."

"That's old business." Simon shrugged dismissively, but he released Bailey's arm and waited for Seven to catch up with them.

The crewmen walked back onto the yacht, smoking cigarettes and talking quietly to themselves as Seven walked toward Bailey and the two men.

"Is Mama home?" Seven asked.

Simon shook his head. "She's still at work."

Seven nodded. He carried two bags with him, including her red overnight case. Bailey looked pointedly at him, then at the bags.

"Later," he murmured.

Later? What did that mean? Not only had the man kidnapped her, he'd brought her to another country, a place where she knew no one and was completely at his mercy. But, watching the easy camaraderie between Seven and his family, and both men's disarming grins, which were so much like Seven's, she knew that on this island, nothing would happen to her that she did not want. She felt safe.

Bailey flicked a glance at Seven, who walked with an even more relaxed stride, body easy and unencumbered in khaki shorts and a plain white T-shirt. He was at home here, and it showed.

They trekked along the path through the dense bushes, passing through a small field of sugar cane, the thick stalks like bamboo, waving against the deep blue sky. The sun burned fiercely overhead, roasting her back and shoulders as she walked with the men. They smelled like sweat and work, of the outdoors. Sweat popped out on her forehead as she walked with them, soaking her back under the thin tank top, the line between her breasts. And it hadn't even seemed that hot. None of the men were even winded. They took the incline, which became more and more pronounced with each step, breathing evenly while Bailey labored for each breath she took on the short walk.

Soon, the field of cane gave way to a wide patch of fruit trees, then low grass as they turned around a bend. A house appeared out of the green.

The first thing Bailey noticed was the garden. Large and brightly colored, it tumbled down the hillside on one side of the porch, bursting with bright orange ginger plants, purple hibiscus and pink bromeliads. On the other side of the steps, an explosion of fruits and vegetables grew—red tomatoes, yellow pumpkins, green zucchini. The house itself was a small white cottage. A few short steps led from the yard up to the wide porch, where half a dozen chairs were scattered in happy profusion, padded and well used, as if the family sat in them every day.

She followed the two men to the porch, where she sat down at their invitation to catch her breath. Bailey fanned herself with a folded-up newspaper from one of the chairs, stirring up the sweat on her face and neck. Simon and his father disappeared into the house, while Seven plopped into a seat next to her.

"It well hot, man," he said to no one in particular.

Winston came back to the porch with a glass of water for Bailey.

"Thank you." She put the cold water to her lips and sighed in relief. This was just what she needed. The cool liquid washed down her throat, dispersing the heat that had been gathering in her on the walk from the pier.

Seven looked up. "What about me?"

"You're not a guest."

Seven sucked his teeth and stayed sagged in the chair. A faint smile tugged at his lips.

"The garden looks good, Papa. Have you eaten anything from it yet?"

"Yes, man. Some sweet potatoes and such. The pumpkin them sweet."

Seven looked up at his father. "You cooking?"

The older man laughed. "Yes. And your mother left a sweet potato pudding for you on the table. She just finished it yesterday, when she thought you'd be here."

"You had a good reason not to rush, brother." Simon came back on the porch with two bottles of Heineken. He gave one to Seven and sat down on the steps with the other. After a moment, he tilted back to look at Bailey. "Did you want to a beer, too?"

She shook her head. "No, thanks. Don't like the taste."

He nodded, as if she confirmed an opinion he already had, and fell into silence as he stared out into the richly green front yard and drank his beer.

After a moment, Seven stood up and touched her shoulder. On the ground by the chair he'd just left, the beer was half-empty.

"Let me show you to your room," he said.

His brother snickered. "What else you going show her in there?"

"Don't you have a house of your own to be at, brother?" Seven looked over his shoulder at Simon.

"It's a house, not a prison. I can visit my parents if I feel like it." Simon laughed and drank more of his beer.

He looked the very image of an old-fashioned demented scientist, with his wild beard, round spectacles and white teeth glinting in the light of the sun.

As Bailey stood up, Seven walked up to the front steps of the porch and not so gently nudged Simon with his knee. The other man laughed harder, clutching his beer to stop it from spilling.

"Seven, we put some towels for you in the guest room," Winston Carmichael said, a soft warning in his voice. "Once you show Bailey the place, come back out here."

Bailey fought a smile. They were protecting her honor. That endeared them to her even more.

"All right, Papa." A thread of petulance laced Seven's voice.

He touched the small of her back and led her into the house.

"Your family is sweet. I like them."

Seven made a soft noise. "Wait until you meet my mother. You might change your mind."

"You think she won't like me?"

Seven chuckled. "I'm joking," he said. "Mama will be a better host than those two." He jerked his head toward the porch, where his brother and father sat.

The sound of their voices in soft conversation floated back to Bailey. She wondered if they were talking about her. She wondered if they knew everything. Her cheeks warmed at the memory of making love with him on the boat. The shameless way she had gripped his hardness inside her, urging him on with the twist of her hips while his hand—

"You'll be sleeping here." Seven stopped to open a door on the right side of the hallway, and Bailey almost ran into his back. She touched his hip to catch her balance and immediately moved back, glad he was in front of her and couldn't see how flustered she was.

The room was small and well lit, with windows on two of the four walls. Its look was masculine but warm, with sage-green walls, tall bookshelves between each window and a dark wooden full-size bed sitting on the alternating-black-and-white-tile floors. A towel, facecloth and bar of soap lay in the middle of the bed.

"Is this your room?"

"Yes. I'm taking the guest room while we're here. This one is more comfortable and closer to the bathroom." He put her overnight bag on the bed.

He moved toward the door but Bailey blocked his way, shutting the door behind her, closing them in. "So just how long are we here for?"

"I'd planned for three days."

"Three days?" Bailey's mouth dropped open. "I can't be gone from work for that long. It's already been too long. Tomorrow is Wednesday!"

"Bette is taking care of it."

"This is crazy!"

Seven put a finger to his lips. "Shh."

"Don't shush me!" Bailey hissed. But she lowered her voice anyway. "My job means something to me. I know you have no idea what I'm talking about, but this is a commitment that I've made. This is important."

"Bette is taking care of it," he said again. He touched her arms, making soothing motions against her bare skin.

"Most days my sister can't even take care of herself,"

Bailey spat. She pulled away from his touch. "Five days from work? I haven't missed a day since I started there."

"Don't you think you're entitled to take a few now?"

Bailey growled with frustration. "The messed-up thing is I don't think you care. This is all some grand adventure to you. You damn so-called free spirits with no concept of real life!" She clenched her fist and held it against her thigh to stop herself from slapping him.

"Is everything okay in here?"

Winston Carmichael's voice came from the other side of the door. Bailey flushed with embarrassment, turning sharply away from Seven.

"Things are fine, Papa."

Bailey felt his eyes on her but didn't turn around.

"Then come out here. I need help getting some vegetables out of the garden for dinner."

"All right. I'm coming."

Bailey turned away from the window to find him watching her.

"The boat is gone," he said. "It won't be back here until Friday. If you want to call your office, you can use the phone here. There's one in the living room." His voice was soft, not placating, simply relaying information.

She didn't need him to remind her that she was the one who'd insisted on them making this journey. If it hadn't been for her, they'd both be in Miami in their separate homes by now. Bailey said nothing. Seven waited for a moment, then two, before he opened the door and left her alone in the room.

Chapter 17

It was too late to go back. On the boat, Seven had been willing and ready to turn around and head to Miami. It was what she wanted. At least that was what he'd thought.

In Key West, her emotional wounds had begun to bleed. Although she hadn't said much about her pain, it was easy to see. Her childhood hurts. Dead parents. Regret for things she had no control over. And he had been the cause of those painful memories resurfacing.

Regret didn't begin to cover what he felt. But when he had gone to her room to apologize and turn the boat around, she'd touched him. In that moment, the familiar throb of desire had sunk into his belly, and he'd wanted to continue his chase, wherever it would lead. And then she'd said, "Lead on."

It had been too late to change her mind. Seven had refocused on his goal, and only one thing would stop him: accomplishing it.

He left her in his old room, filled with an odd sort of regret. He didn't want to hurt her. He didn't want to be the kind of man she described with her biting words. He *wasn't* that man. But how would he show her that?

"What you doing in there with that girl?" his father asked as soon as he came out to the veranda.

"If you have to ask him, you're too old." Simon laughed

from his crouch in the garden at their father's side. He dug carefully around a vine to get to the yam in the dirt.

"He better not be doing that in there. Your mama won't have it."

"I know, Papa. We were just talking." Seven reclaimed his chair and the Heineken.

"Right." Simon scoffed.

Seven threw a narrow-eyed gaze at his brother.

His father dropped a newly unearthed potato into the basket at his feet. "You never did tell us what you're doing down here. We thought you were going to be in the desert for a while."

"The desert is too dry for me. I had to get close to some water." Seven sipped his beer.

"You can always move back home," his father said. "Your mother would love to see you back here."

Ever since they had semiretired and moved back to Jamaica from the States, his parents seemed to have erased any memory of being away from the island. They bought land close to where they both had been born and built a house on it. In the house, they kept rooms waiting for Seven and Simon whenever they visited, acting as though these rooms had sheltered the boys through their childhoods, when in fact they'd spent most of their youth in Brooklyn, New York, in the heart of the Jamaican community.

"They haven't offered me any work here, Papa," Seven said. "If they did, I'd think about it."

Simon scoffed again. He wiped dirt from the yams and potatoes he'd pulled from the ground, supposedly what their father had called Seven to do. He dumped them in the basket, his neatly manicured doctor's hands smeared with the brown soil. Simon didn't mind it. As one of the leading research epidemiologists at the University of the West Indies, he played with microscopes, computer keyboards and data all day. Seven knew it was rare enough for his brother to be at their parents' house, and rarer still for him to be working in their garden.

"What are you doing so far from the university, Simon? Don't you have to be at work tomorrow?"

"You blind, you see it's still today?"

"Chuh, man! Why yu a gw'aan so?"

"Some woman," his father said. "The same reason you're acting foolish, too."

Seven looked at his twin. "I thought you were going to ask Winsome to marry you."

"I did. She said she had to think about it."

"Well, that's a long and drawn out no if I ever heard one."

"That's what I said." Winston stood up and brushed off his knees. "When I asked your mother to marry me, she said yes. No 'let me think about it and weigh my options.' She knew and I knew that we were going to be together."

"Not everybody can be as certain as you, Papa." Simon grimaced and looked at Seven. "Is that girl in there certain she wants to marry you?"

Seven almost choked on his beer. "Marry? What are you talking about?"

"You and that Bailey girl." He repeated himself as if Seven was particularly slow. "Why else would you bring a girl home to meet your parents unless you wanted to marry her?"

When he'd first thought about bringing Bailey to Jamaica, he was going to book them in adjoining rooms at a resort near his parents' house. But Bette had encouraged him to stay with his parents, tug on her sister's heartstrings and pull her toward him that much faster. Her deviousness on his behalf had surprised Seven, but he'd immediately changed his plans. He wondered now if he had made a tactical error.

"Who are you going to marry?" a female voice called up from the front yard.

Seven looked away from his brother's laughing gaze to see Millicent Carmichael walking up the path to the house.

"How you hear that from way back there, Mama?" Seven stood up and left his beer on the floor. A grin split his face as he jogged down the steps and swept his mother up in a big hug.

At fifty-nine, she was a vibrant and strong woman with purple-black skin and a stout and practical shape that never changed the whole time Seven had known her. Despite the afternoon heat, she wore a lightweight blue coat over her nurse's uniform and held a brown purse in the crook of her arm.

"Don't try to change the subject, boy." She scowled, but the look in her eyes was pure love. After suffering through six stillborn and miscarried children, she would always see him as her miracle boy. Her first, though not her last. "Is it the girl you brought?"

"Simon thinks so."

"He's not stupid, so there must be something to what he's talking about."

Seven kept his arm around his mother's shoulder as they walked up the steps to the veranda. He hadn't told his family much about his relationship with Bailey, or even about Bailey herself, but obviously they had speculated.

"I just wanted to bring her out on a vacation, Mama. Where else is the perfect vacation place but Jamaica?"

"She lives in Miami, right?"

Seven laughed ruefully. "Right."

On the veranda, she looked around her. "Where is this girl? I thought you said you brought her here with you."

"I did. She's in my room."

His mother gave him a sharp look.

"She's staying in there by herself," he said quickly.

"She better." His mother took off her jacket and draped it over her arm as she walked into the house. Inside the front door, she put her purse on the table and her jacket over the peg by the door.

"Your father is cooking tonight." She looked at her reflection in the mirror over the table, smoothed a hand down the front of her uniform, which was still clean despite a long day at the hospital. "But I made you something sweet. Just in case."

"Papa told me about the pudding."

"Cho man!" A look of irritation crossed her face. "That man! Always ruining my surprises." She walked down the wide hallway toward her room, but instead of continuing, she stopped at Seven's old room and knocked.

"Mama…" he warned. But she ignored him.

A moment later, Bailey came to the door. Her eyes were red, as if she'd been crying, the front of her tank top and shorts wrinkled from lying on the bed. Her hair was a wild halo around her head. After a brief look at Seven, she avoided his gaze.

He felt like a complete ass. That look on her face was because of him.

"Hello, young lady." His mother looked Bailey over, not missing a thing.

"Mrs. Carmichael?" Bailey smoothed a hand down the front of her shorts.

"I am Seven's mother, yes."

Bailey took his mother's hand between her own, no sign of the angry woman he had left not too long before. "Thank you so much for welcoming me into your home. I heard about the pudding. I'm excited to taste it."

Millicent Carmichael looked at Seven over her shoulder. "She's a nice one." To Bailey, she said, "Wash your face and come out to the veranda, darlin' dear. I'm going to wash the day off this tired old body and sit down with pudding and brandy. Come out with me."

The not-quite-a-request didn't seem to faze Bailey. "I'd love to, Mrs. Carmichael."

"Call me Mrs. Millicent, child. Mrs. Carmichael is my husband's late mother, God rest her soul."

Then she backed out of the room and turned to Seven. "Make sure she has everything she needs." She guided him not so subtly into the room, then closed the door, shutting him inside with Bailey.

He cleared his throat, uncertain what to say. Bailey looked at him with her reddened eyes. Then, when the silence became unbearable, he finally spoke. "You don't need anything, do you?"

"No." Her tone was cold. Uninviting.

Seven cleared his throat again. "I…I do know that your job is important to you. And I care about that. Your future at the firm is not in danger, I promise." He lifted a hand to touch her arm but changed his mind in midmotion and dropped it back to his side. "Call your office if you don't believe me. I didn't bring you here to ruin your life. Just to share some of mine with you."

"You're going about it in a really messed-up way," she said.

She was thawing. He could feel it. He could see it in the way she uncrossed her arms, tucked her hands in the pockets of her shorts. Relief trickled slowly through him.

"There's no script for life, Bailey. I'm just going after what I want. You should do the same."

"I am. Partner at the firm, remember?"

His mouth twitched, but not in amusement. "How could I forget? You're willing to do a lot for that partnership. If they hadn't sent you after me as a client, would we have anything to say to each other? Or more to the point, would you have anything to say to me?"

She bit her lip. "I'm not compromising my integrity for them, Seven. I would never do that."

"That's not what I said."

"But that's what you implied."

"It's what you feel you've done," he gently insisted.

She pressed her lips together and said nothing, only hugged herself around her middle and watched him with her narrow, expressive eyes. "All I've ever wanted is security. When I was a child, I had none. My family and I lived the most exciting life ever, but we didn't know what was going to happen at the end of Daddy's fellowship or Mama's residency. At one point we were even on government assistance. I don't want to go back to that. I need to feel safe."

"But don't you want to be happy, too?"

"Yes," she cried with frustration. "That partnership will buy me all the happiness and security I need."

"And will being a partner to two old men in a high-rise downtown keep your bed warm at night?"

She flinched. "I think you're out of line," she said coldly.

"How can I be out of line when I dream about you damn near every night? How can I be out of line when every time I look at you, all I remember is the way your body feels on top of mine—the noises you made when I was inside you." Unable to help himself, he stepped closer. "Do you remember?"

He watched the smooth column of her throat as she swallowed again, watched her uncross her arms and begin to back away from him.

"I never forgot," she said, her voice a husky vibration between them.

Seven moved closer until he felt the heat from her body burning into his in waves. She had to tilt her head up to look at him. Her breath brushed against his throat, his cheek. He stepped closer and she took the final step into him. Her arms flew up around his neck, body crushed against his, her mouth open and eager.

Yes. His blood thundered in his ears. *Yes.*

She tasted of the sea and of tears, salt and damp and sad. He drank her up, explored the soft space of her mouth with his tongue, trying to sweep away the sadness he tasted there.

"I didn't mean to hurt you," he murmured against her mouth. Seven pulled her closer and closer still. He still couldn't enough of her sweet mouth, the heat of her skin against his.

She moaned and he was lost. He maneuvered her backward toward the bed. They tilted but he held her, an arm lashed around her back, the other braced against the bed to gentle their fall to the mattress. His mouth devoured hers, and her fingernails raked the back of his head and neck. Her thighs widened under him and he fell between them, grateful. Hot. Hard.

She moaned again and he grabbed her hips, jerking her up hard against him as he moved against her.

"God!" he groaned against her throat. "I want to—" He fumbled with the edge of her shirt, unable to articulate what he wanted. His pulse was like a runaway train. "Can I?"

"Yes," she said breathlessly.

Seven yanked up her tank top and her bra and buried his face in her skin, mouth falling in worship on her breasts, tasting her, sucking until she writhed under him, her nails sinking into his back, his butt, his thighs.

She gasped his name. The sound of it on her lips jerked through him, ratcheting his arousal even higher. Christ! He had to have her. He felt the heat of her center against him through her shorts even as her breasts in his mouth pulled any rational thought from his brain.

"I need you," she breathed.

Bailey arched up against him, moaning his name as her hips made hot, erotic circles under him. She shoved down her shorts and panties, and he touched her, felt the wetness and heat of her and how she wanted him. His head nearly exploded.

"I need you," she said again and bit his ear.

Seven unzipped his shorts. He fumbled between them to get rid of all the barriers to them both getting what they wanted.

From far away, he heard a knock, then a voice call out. "Seven, are you— Oh!"

The bedroom door opened. Then slammed shut.

He jackknifed off her. "Dammit!" He yanked up his shorts and carefully zipped himself up, pulse out of control, loins like molten iron. Seven cursed bad timing, cursed his runaway libido. "I'm sorry," he said between his teeth. "I'm sorry."

He cursed again, then leaned his hot forehead against the closed door, panting, trying to get himself under control. Swallowing heavily, he turned, then wished he hadn't.

Bailey lay sprawled on the bed, where he'd left her, thighs spread wide, her tank top and bra shoved up to show her small, tempting breasts, their heaving peaks still wet from his mouth. Her lips looked thoroughly kissed. Her hair was a lust-mussed mess. He wanted to crawl back to her and devour every inch of her body. He swallowed again. Then looked away. Clasped his hand around the doorknob.

"Come out to the veranda when you can. Mama will be waiting for you."

He walked out.

Chapter 18

With the flush of arousal gone, Bailey felt humiliated. She lay on the bed, the front of her still warm from the press of Seven's body against hers. His mother's face over his shoulder had been a study in embarrassment and a strange satisfaction.

"Damn."

She shoved her hands through her hair and got up from the bed. Instead of washing her face like Mrs. Millicent had suggested, she needed a shower. A nice, cold one.

After a brief search, she found the bathroom in the hall, grateful that she didn't run into anyone on her way to it.

Once showered, she scurried back into the bedroom, covered by the thin, white robe she'd found near the bed. Although she felt like wearing another pair of shorts and tank top in deference to the heat, she pulled on her jeans and a cap-sleeved white blouse from her bag and put them on. Maybe since she was so covered up, his mother wouldn't remember that she'd seen Bailey damn near naked under Seven, begging him to take her. *Right*.

She groaned again in embarrassment. How could she have let things get that far? But the question was moot. Things had gotten that far, and even now, she could say only that she regretted his mother had found them so soon. Another fifteen minutes—or hour—was all she'd have needed.

She had to laugh at herself. Bette would laugh at her, too. Imagine her, losing her mind over some man.

Granted, Seven was not just any man. He was the sexiest creature she'd ever met, wooing her with his sense of humor as much as with his body. Under different circumstances, or perhaps in another life, she would have already taken him to meet her sister and tried for something more permanent. But every action of his had proved what she thought about him. He was irresponsible. Just a younger version of her father.

She opened the door and left the room.

The entire family was on the porch. Simon and Winston Carmichael had cleaned themselves up, or at least washed the dirt from their hands and faces, while Mrs. Millicent had changed into a light orange-colored dress and open-toed house slippers. She sat in the chair closest to the right railing. A coffee table was in front of her, and a small, covered cake dish, along with five small plates and forks, claimed its center.

"Come sit here next to me," Mrs. Millicent said when she noticed Bailey hesitating in the doorway. She patted the rattan chair next to hers. There was no judgment in her face about what she had seen earlier, just a touch of…pity?

Only once she was sitting down did Bailey allow herself to look at Seven. He hadn't changed his clothes. He hadn't washed. He wore the same thing he'd had on when he'd pressed her into the mattress, the strong heat of his sex hard against her. Helpless color scorched her cheeks.

"Was the water pressure okay?" Mrs. Millicent asked.

"Yes, it was fine. Very strong." The cool water had blasted against her with a surprising force, shocking her skin.

"It was very weak a few days ago. I asked Simon to take care of it. As usual, he does more than enough and I feel flagellated every time I use that shower. Thank God it's not very often. I prefer a bath."

"I didn't mind it." She nodded at Seven's brother, who watched her with a smirk. "Better strong than weak," she said.

"Amen to that," Winston said.

Mrs. Millicent glanced at her husband with an amused smile. "Would you like some of the potato pudding?" she asked Bailey.

"Yes, please. It's been awhile since I ate."

"Really? Seven usually feeds his women better than that." Mrs. Millicent removed the cover of the cake pan, revealing thick squares of what looked like bread pudding.

With a fork, she slid one onto each plate and passed one to Bailey first, then to her men.

"I wasn't that hungry, actually," she said, in a rush to defend Seven, although she wasn't sure if she liked being referred to as one of his women. How many had there been? Did he bring all of them home? "He took very good care of me during the ride from Miami." She saw Seven and his brother exchange a look. "He's a great cook and an even better man. You raised a wonderful son." Bailey stopped, not sure why she'd added that last bit. But as she watched Seven trying to juggle his beer and the slice of pudding his mother had passed to him, she acknowledged just how true that was.

He had been kind, generous and intuitive. A gentleman. She could have been kidnapped by worse. The thought made her smile.

"Well, that's a good sign, Seven." Simon tilted his fork toward his brother. "He was out here saying how much he offended you earlier and that he might have to find a way to get you back to that boat."

She felt all four pairs of eyes on her, waiting for her response. Bailey decided to tread with caution but honesty, as well. "It's true that we had a disagreement, but that's no reason for us to rush off." She smiled at Mrs. Millicent. "I'm enjoying my time here."

"Good, dear. That's very good."

She thought she saw Seven slump the tiniest bit with relief in his chair.

Mrs. Millicent poured a glass of brandy for herself, then for Bailey. "This is a pretty drink," Seven's mother said. "I wouldn't be surprised if a woman invented it."

Winston chuckled from his place on the porch. He had a slice of the pudding on his knee but did not touch it. "Not only women make pretty things, Milly. Look at Seven and his work. Some of that stuff is what you'd call pretty."

"Art is something else entirely," she said, taking a sip of her drink. She sighed with pleasure. "Our son makes beautiful art because he's a beautiful soul."

"I think you're a little biased on both counts, my dear."

Seven leaned back in his chair. "You don't think I have a beautiful soul, Papa?" His tone was light, teasing, as if they'd talked about this topic more than once.

"I'll leave matters of aesthetics up to your mother." Winston bowed out of the discussion gracefully.

Mrs. Millicent turned to Bailey. "What do you think, my dear? Does my son make beautiful art?"

Bailey felt her cheeks grow warm again. She was apparently going to spend all her time with Seven's family with her face burning with embarrassment. "Actually, I—" She fingered the glass of brandy.

"I haven't shown her anything of mine yet, Mama."

"Why?" His mother seemed so genuinely confused that Bailey smiled. "I know you're proud of your work. We all are."

"I know, Mama. I know."

Simon forked a piece of the pudding to his mouth. "It actually took us all a while to be proud of Seven. Wasting time on something that wasn't guaranteed to be lucrative is pretty much taboo in Jamaica. Most of the artists on the island come from well-off families, so they can afford not to make money. Not my brother."

Bailey watched Seven's face, saw the vague discomfort at being the topic of conversation.

"I knew I could always mooch off my doctor brother if things didn't work out," he said.

Bailey doubted that very much. She hadn't known the man for very long, but he didn't seem the type to depend on his family. When they first met, she'd expected him to be at all of Marcus's parties, where the women and booze ran freely for anyone in his inner circle. But other than the two parties where she'd run into him, Bailey hadn't heard of him taking advantage of Marcus the way others had. And he definitely wasn't in the douche-bag category, as she'd first assumed. He was just Seven, the man who was a number.

"You'd have to come back to Jamaica to mooch off us, and I know you don't want to live back on the island," Mrs. Millicent said.

Curious, Bailey looked at Seven. "Why don't you want to live here?"

He shrugged. "I don't want to get killed over some stupidness."

"The crime here is very bad," Mr. Carmichael explained. "People kill over nothing here. Dominoes. A sandwich." He glanced at Simon. "Sometimes we worry for our other son."

"I love Jamaica," Simon murmured. "Nothing can make me leave again." He jerked his chin dismissively. "Besides, around here it's very peaceful. The most that can happen is stubbing your toe walking down to the beach in the dark."

"We raised our boys in America. After Simon graduated from medical school, he moved back here to do his residency."

Simon made a noise. "No one wants to hear about that, Mama." He threw his head back to finish the last of his beer. "Who wants to play dominoes?"

They played dominoes for the rest of the afternoon, sitting around a well-used wooden table. The men played fiercely, cursing each other good-naturedly, while Mrs. Millicent and Bailey took a more low-key but just as ruthless route. The sky's color faded around them, changing from the brightest blue to orange-brushed aquamarine, and finally to indigo.

As darkness came, and it looked as if Mrs. Millicent would win the latest game, Winston threw down his dominoes.

"Time for me to make dinner," he said, then disappeared into the house.

"Let me know if you need any help," Mrs. Millicent called after her husband. His infectious laughter flowed out to them. Mrs. Millicent looked at the tiles in her hands. "Why don't you take Bailey and show her around, Seven?" She didn't look up from the game.

"It's too dark to show her anything," Seven said.

"The night often reveals things we can't see in the day," she said.

Simon nodded, a faint smile on his mouth.

"Besides, you know I'm winning anyway," his mother said.

Seven made a sound of frustration. "True." Mrs. Millicent had trounced them in the last two hands. "Okay." He dropped his tiles to the table. "Bailey?"

His mother's face gave nothing away. She merely studied the tiles on the table, not looking at anyone else. Was she trying to tell them something? Bailey wondered. But another look at Seven's mother revealed nothing. She stood up, leaving her tiles on the table. "Sure."

She didn't take his hand, although he offered it. Only followed him down the steps and out into the night, which was darker than any she'd seen in a long time. Because of the lack of streetlights, skyscrapers or cars, the stars were brilliant above them. Bailey looked up, trying to remember her father's lessons on the stars, to recall which was the Big Dipper, which was Orion's Belt. It always amazed her that people on different continents, thousands of miles apart, were able to look up at the same stars. Miraculous.

They walked in silence for long moments, Seven's quiet breathing next to her, the sound of their footsteps along the path leading from the house and the way they had come earlier that day. Voices emerged from the night before them, then a soft glow. Someone's flashlight. Soon, a couple walked down the path in their direction, a man and a woman talking softly together.

"Evening," Seven greeted them.

The couple called out the same and kept walking. She wondered where they were going. Wondered if the path behind her and Seven would take them to the beach and then into the intimate shelter of each other's arms.

"I think your mother is trying to tell us something," she finally said.

Seven chuckled. "You think so?" Their feet crunched on the gravel road. Crickets chirped in the darkness. "She knows we had a disagreement. Before, she was trying to make sure that we made up."

Yes, they'd made up, all right. Bailey got warm under her clothes thinking about the ways they'd "made up" in his room. Her palms itched with the urge to make up with him now.

"And what's her reason for sending us out in the dark?"

"Maybe she just wants one of her children to give her grandsons ASAP."

"Not funny," she said.

He laughed again. "If you say so. But it is a perfect night for outdoor sex. What else do you think those two back there were heading for?"

So, he had been thinking about that couple, as well.

"What they're doing has nothing to do with us."

"You're right. You're absolutely right." He paused. "For the record, I am sorry about what happened back there in my room. I mean, I'm not sorry I kissed you or…"

His words trailed off, conjuring for Bailey the images of the other things he had done, that they had done together. His mouth on her breasts. Her thighs clasping him, clinging. His heat against her heat.

"I'm sorry that my mother burst in and embarrassed you," Seven finished.

"I was embarrassed, at first," Bailey said. "But your mother, she treated it like it was nothing." Bailey looked up at him. "She's very unusual."

"She's always been understanding about everything. She gave my brother and me a good amount of leeway growing up, but she didn't let us get away with anything ridiculous, either."

"That sounds nice," Bailey murmured.

He laughed. "Not when you're a teenage boy and want to get away with everything under the sun." His laughter misted out into the night, wrapping around her like the coziest of blankets.

"Like what?" she asked, meeting his lingering smile with her own. "What did you and Simon do as kids?"

"The real question is, what did we *not* do?" Seven chuck-led. "One time…"

Bailey leaned closer to hear the story.

Chapter 19

Bailey smiled at Seven as they finished their walk at the steps to his parents' house. His mother sat in her chair, lightly fanning herself, feet up as she looked into the night.

"She's something, sweet, nuh," his mother remarked with a satisfied light in her eyes, watching the two of them.

"Just like honey," Seven responded.

Millicent Carmichael laughed out loud. Her fan slowed. "Dinner is almost ready. Simon is washing up, you two should do the same."

His father had made ackee and saltfish, with the Irish potatoes and pumpkin from the garden, along with dumplings and boiled bananas. A favorite of Seven's. His mother blessed the food and they began to eat.

During dinner, he watched Bailey. Glowing and fresh from their walk, she looked more relaxed than ever. He couldn't keep his eyes off her. She was the magnet to his steel, the flower to his hummingbird. The water for his thirst. He wanted her so badly he could taste it. He wanted to taste *her*. Instead, he drank deeply from his glass of water.

"Did you enjoy your walk in our little neighborhood, Bailey?" his mother asked.

"Yes, Mrs. Millicent, I did. There wasn't much to see

by starlight, but your son was a very entertaining guide." Her eyes met Seven's across the table. She was smiling.

"Good. This boy of mine could make an anthill seem interesting with the way he tells a story." She jerked her chin toward Simon. "And that other one would dissect the whole thing to show you how it worked."

The pride in her voice made Seven sit up a little taller, and he felt his brother do the same.

When they were growing up, his parents had never skimped on their compliments, always letting Simon and Seven know they were proud, that they loved them and that the boys could do anything. Some days, he thought his parents' love and complete acceptance were the reasons he'd come so far in his work. They believed. He believed. He achieved.

After dinner, he washed the dishes, and though he wanted to pursue Bailey and take her away somewhere quiet to talk, he let her go off with his mother to talk about American politics and race and anything else Millicent Carmichael came up with. Instead, he went in search of Simon, who was staying at their parents' house yet again. His brother was in his bedroom, looking at something on his laptop when Seven walked in. Simon glanced up from his work.

"Your girl is fire, man." His brother closed the computer and looked up at Seven with a smirk.

"She is." Seven sat at the head of the bed, leaning back against the headboard. "I thought you had a hot one of your own."

Simon made a dismissive noise. "Winsome is too ghetto, man."

Seven laughed. "But didn't you ask her to marry you?"

"Yes. And she just about turned me down."

"As if she's going to catch another doctor, with the way

she acts up." Seven raised an eyebrow. "She's playing more games?"

"When is she not playing games?" Simon put the computer aside and sat next to Seven against the headboard. "That's what I get for running after a Spanish Town girl."

"Plenty of girls in Spanish Town are sane. You just found the wrong one."

His brother turned to him as if to defend the sanity of the woman he'd chosen to marry, but he only looked at Seven with frustration pinching the corners of his eyes. In the end, he couldn't say anything.

"When you first got with her I thought you were crazy, too. Remember that night she burst into the kitchen, saying she was going to show Papa how to cook?" Seven chuckled. "Mama almost threw her out on her butt."

"It was a long time before she got invited back to dinner again." Simon nodded, smiling. "She *is* crazy, but that's one of the things I love about her. And she's amazing in bed."

The men shared a rough, masculine laugh.

"As long as you're getting something out of her other than headaches, man."

"I get plenty, don't you worry."

They laughed again.

"Is that what's up with you and that American girl? She has plenty of fire but seems to run a little cold."

Seven thought for a moment before answering. Although it had been only a few weeks, his pursuit of Bailey was coming to mean more than it should have. He wanted more than just sex from her. Aside from the wild, sheet-tearing passion they'd already shared, he just plain liked her. There weren't many people he could say that about.

"I want her to have my babies," Seven finally said.

And he wasn't exactly joking.

Chapter 20

Bailey wanted him. But she knew that she couldn't, shouldn't, have him. Seven was the finest example of a man that she'd ever met. And his parents loved him, supported him and were extraordinary in their own way. But he still wasn't the man for her. His career relied too much on chance. He was reckless. He'd kidnapped her, for God's sake!

Unable to deal with the never-ending conversations pulsing in her head, she left the house to go for a walk. She needed to clear her mind. Mr. and Mrs. Carmichael had already left for work, and Seven was paying a brief visit to his brother's house in Kingston to pick "something" up. Though left alone, Bailey could no longer stay in the house.

She didn't know where she was going, but from the walk she and Seven had taken the night before, she remembered certain details of the small town.

In the daylight, the town was green, expansive and strangely beautiful. It was scattered here and there with tin-roofed huts, charming cottages like the one the Carmichaels lived in, even large, multilevel minimansions. The main road had tiny lanes shooting off from it, leading uphill into hidden paths bursting with wild growths of red hibiscus and bright yellow and orange ginger plants with their bristled coxcomb petals. It was lovely. She could see why the Carmichaels loved it.

Bailey had been to Jamaica once with her parents when she was a child, but didn't remember very much of the experience. Only the strange accents and the endless summer fruit she and Bette had eaten until they were stuffed.

A teasing wind ruffled Bailey's loose hair, brushing the thick, frizzy mop against her shoulders.. The wind molded the dress to the front of her body, whipped the wide skirts behind her like a flag.

Up the road, two men and a woman walked toward her, talking excitedly. The woman was pretty. Thick and a deep milk chocolate, she wore her long, permed hair in a ponytail, had on navy shorts and a black T-shirt advertising a cell phone company. Her male companions were shirtless and wore shorts.

When they noticed her, the conversation stopped. The woman stared hard at Bailey as she came closer.

"You," she said when Bailey was only a few feet away.

"I guess." Bailey shrugged. "I'm always me."

"I heard you were out walking with the Carmichael boy the other night."

Bailey looked at her. She'd never heard anyone refer to Seven as "the Carmichael boy" in her life, but that *was* his last name.

"It was a nice night."

The woman actually snarled. "Stay the hell away from him, he's my man!"

Bailey couldn't have heard right. "What?"

"You heard me, bitch!"

The men watched their friend with admiration while Bailey stared. "Are you serious? I just got here from Miami and now you're threatening me over some man?"

The woman snapped her fingers a few feet from Bailey's face. "He's not some man, he's my man, and you better stay away."

Bailey shook her head. "I can kiss——" she deliberately used the word to see the woman's furious expression grow "——any man I want to. If he wanted you, obviously he wouldn't have been with me."

Seven had a woman in Jamaica? She was never the type to fight for a man, and she sure as hell wasn't about to start now.

"Bitch, you better——" The woman bucked at Bailey only to have her two friends laughingly pull her back.

"Leave the gyal alone." The young man in khaki shorts spoke up. "If you want the man, just take him. He's not playing hard to get. He let you know plenty of times he would marry you if you gave him the chance."

The woman sucked her teeth, still trying to get at Bailey from the strong grip on both of her arms. "Back off!" she called out.

Bailey was getting annoyed. "You back off! If you want him so bad, how come he's not with you?"

"Because your American pum pum turn him into a fool!"

"What?" Bailey shook her head, truly annoyed now.

The day's beauty had dried up in the face of the woman's rudeness and wild claims. Who the hell attacked a stranger just because they suspected someone was trying to steal their man? This woman was really stupid.

Growing up, Bailey had been witness to some truly ridiculous behavior—girls willing to go to jail or the hospital over guys who wouldn't spit on them if they were on fire. That was so damn simpleminded.

She wasn't about to get caught up in that, no matter how fine Seven was. Bailey gave the girl a narrow-eyed glance.

"You should check your man, not me," she said. Then she walked past the girl and her keepers to head back toward the house.

* * *

When she got back to the Carmichaels' house, Seven was already back and waiting for her on the veranda. Wearing a much-washed white T-shirt that was nearly transparent over his muscular chest, knee-length blue plaid shorts and sandals, he was the very picture of relaxation. He looked satisfied. Happy.

"Where have you been?" he asked, looking up from the newspaper he was reading.

"Taking a walk."

Bailey wasn't particularly in the mood to talk about what had happened out there with that woman. It still felt so damn unreal. Some strange woman confronting her about a man? Even thinking it sounded ridiculous.

The newspaper in Seven's hand rustled as he looked carefully over her face, frowning. "It must not have been a very peaceful walk. You look a little riled up."

Riled up was an understatement.

"I'm fine." She made an effort to control the hardness in her voice that threatened to smash through their civilized conversation. "Did you get what you went into town for?"

"Yes, as a matter of fact." He tossed the newspaper down in the chair next to him. "Are you ready for a field trip?"

"Field trip?"

"Yeah. To get out of here for a while. Take in some new scenery. I love my parents and their house, but I know that after a while, this rural scene can seem a little too sedentary. Especially for someone who grew up in a city like Miami."

"It's been wonderful here. I haven't been bored once."

Seven was still for a moment, watching her with a small smile curving his lips. "Of course you would feel that way," he said. "You are my mother's dream."

"What?"

"Never mind. Let's go." He stood up, pulling a set of keys from his pocket.

While Bailey waited, he locked up the house, then gestured for her to follow him. They left the veranda side by side, waking in silence toward the backyard. There, in a well-maintained shed with a zinc roof, waited an early-model Range Rover truck.

"Get in."

The old SUV smelled faintly of leather cleaner and faded potpourri. The black leather seats were supple and soft under Bailey's thighs. The comfortable confines of the truck were a pleasant respite from the heat. Bailey buckled hear seat belt as Seven checked the mirrors, started the truck. The mellow sounds of a local oldies radio station filled the vehicle.

He didn't say anything, and Bailey wasn't in any hurry to break the silence, either. Soon, they were driving down the back way from the house, then retracing Bailey's earlier steps through the town. Not long after, unfamiliar roads rolled under the tires, an even greener landscape with flowers blooming here and there among the lush forest.

"So, where are we going?"

Seven glanced over at her with that faint smile of his. "A garden not too far from here."

"That's not much of a change of scenery. Your parents have a fantastic garden back at the house."

"This one is a bit more unique than that."

She raised an eyebrow at his smug tone. "This garden better be the most amazing and unique thing I've ever seen in my life."

"Wait a minute, now! I never promised you *that*." He chuckled.

"Make big promises and you get raised expectations." She found herself smiling back at him.

"Damn, I'll have to remember that for next time."

Bantering back and forth with him, Bailey rediscovered the feeling of camaraderie and ease she'd shared with Seven the night before. She purposely pushed the encounter she'd had with the woman on the street to the back of her mind. It was too painful, too confusing to deal with yet. Instead, she focused on the simple pleasure of being with an attractive—though off-limits—man.

Soon, they were driving into a more populated area. Trees cut back. Grass manicured. White stone fences. They passed large squat-shaped houses. They drove past a man riding on his donkey, his bare chest glistening from the morning heat, a red bandanna tied around the plodding donkey's neck. A slim young woman with a basket balanced on her head walked just ahead of him.

The truck pulled into a roundabout. On the other side of the roundabout stood an elegant marble sign bidding welcome to Park of the Maroons. An arched gateway soared over the paved road leading into the park, which reminded Bailey of a European sculpture garden.

Strategically placed all around the acres of green grass were whirling, dancing, looming figures in steel, stone, wire and various other materials. Seven pulled the truck into a parking space near half a dozen other vehicles and turned off the engine.

"Come," he said. "I want to show you something."

He hopped out of the truck, pocketed the keys, then came around to Bailey's side in time to open the door for her and help her out. Instead of releasing her after she stood outside the truck, his arm slipped around her waist and he drew her close to him. The motion was so natural, so unremarkable, that Bailey didn't truly realize what he had done until they were walking, pressed hip to hip, toward a trio of statues.

For a moment, she was overwhelmed by the fresh,

clean smell of him. The hint of sweat combined with a faint sweetness, as if he'd been walking through a field of roses. Bailey simply inhaled him, closing her eyes as they walked together, savoring him in her lungs.

"Careful," he said, his hand tugging her even more against him.

Her eyes flew open in time to see him guide her around a low formation of rocks on the ground—another sculpture. The park was lush and green, the grass a deep and vibrant shade under the bright sun and blue skies. They weren't the only ones enjoying the scenery.

Nearby, a family of three sat on a large blanket. Two women and a little boy. The remains of a picnic lunch were scattered around the blanket. Paper plates, half a sandwich, empty soda bottles. They looked happy. All around them, other families—along with some couples and singles—walked through the winding paths of the sculpture garden, touching the figures with wonder, some laughing or sheepish at the nudity on display in a few of the pieces.

Having been surrounded by art and artists most of her life, Bailey loved art of all kinds. Even with her resentment of her parents and the way they had raised her and Bette, she still loved and respected the immense talent it took to bring something from the imagination into being. Looking around the garden, she saw many beautiful things, and some disturbing things, things she would have never thought possible.

"This is one of my favorite places in Jamaica," Seven said.

He gestured around the park to the art and the people enjoying it. "When I doubt that my work connects with any sort of audience, all I have to do is come here and see how people interact with the pieces."

Bailey nodded, looking even more closely around the

park. He was right. Even those who had been ignoring the art in favor of their own meals or conversations occasionally looked up at a piece and pointed, gaze fluttering over the sculptures that were much more than scenery.

"This is a wonderful place," she said.

Their footsteps moved in sync over the cement walkway, their hips touching, his smell a beautiful intoxicant. Did he "belong" to that woman she had met earlier that day? Would she ever put herself in the position of having to fight for him? The question frightened her. She would never have even asked herself something like that before. The hand in her pocket twitched. Bailey licked her lips and glanced up at Seven. He was already looking down at her.

There was a slight nervousness to him that she hadn't noticed before, as if he was perched on an edge. And waiting. Their footsteps stopped. To distract herself from him and his intense look, Bailey turned to the sculpture closest to them.

It was tall, the apex reaching nearly ten feet high. From where she stood, the piece seemed to be made of steel, of hundreds of connected hands with their fingers spread wide to shape a larger female figure, round hipped, high breasted, hands lifting a laughing girl child toward the heavens. The child reached up for the skies her mother offered to her. The detail in the hands making up the figures was amazing. They were long hands, feminine, with slender fingers and short nails. Bailey noticed that each hand was roughly the same size as hers. She turned away from Seven to look closer at the piece.

It stood on a hip-high marble slab. The title of the piece was etched into a plaque settled into the slab. *The Love She Needs*. Beside it, the name of the artist. Bailey drew in a breath of surprise, turned to him.

"This is yours?"

He nodded. Hands in his pockets, watching her with a deliberately casual look on his face. At once, she knew he wasn't going to ask her what she thought about the work. He simply stood there as if he'd presented his whole heart to her and was waiting for her to slash it to pieces. She turned to look at the woman he had sculpted. She stepped away from him, hand reaching up to touch the cool steel as she walked around the piece. Bailey couldn't imagine the skill, patience and strength it took to create something like this. From the other side of the sculpture, she could see him through the shell of hands, his face closed, that beautiful body of his tense and waiting.

"It's incredible," she said.

She saw him sag minutely, his body admitting relief even though he said nothing. Finally, a smile drifted across his mouth.

"There isn't anything you would have done differently?" he asked.

She didn't look away from him. "No. Everything about this is absolutely perfect."

They spent another hour in the sculpture garden, taking in the work of other Jamaican artists, discussing what they liked about the pieces, what they would buy if they could. After nearly an hour, Bailey pled starvation and they left for a restaurant nearby that was one of Seven's favorites. Over stew peas and oxtail, they talked more and flirted, even had a cocktail or three while they explored the details of their mutual love of art.

"Your work is incredible," she said, playing with the umbrella in her cocktail. "I had no idea." The alcohol had warmed her body. She felt relaxed and at peace with the whole wide world.

"Good." Seven's eyes glittered with a mixture of humor

and pleasure. "If you're impressed by that, wait until you see my—" He glanced down at his crotch.

Bailey laughed, slapping a hand over her mouth to stifle the loud guffaw that instantly attracted the attention of other bar patrons. "I've already seen that."

"And?"

She laughed again.

Bailey lost herself in the rest of the conversation with Seven, letting herself forget about the woman she had encountered earlier that day, enjoying his humor, the passion with which he spoke of the things he loved, even his method of sculpting, which she found surprisingly interesting. Sexy, even. It wasn't long before she pictured him shirtless, welding while sparks flew, his muscles flexing and hard, coated by sweat as he sculpted another of his intricate creations.

All too soon, late afternoon came, then evening. Their drinks wore off and it was time to head back to the house and to what she'd quickly come to accept as a normal evening at the Carmichaels' house. On the way back, they sat on their respective sides of the Range Rover, lost in their separate thoughts.

Bailey couldn't stop staring at Seven, and a few times she'd caught him looking at her. They exchanged smiles, but otherwise kept themselves in the warm cocoon of their own ruminations. Bailey knew she had a lot to think about.

Chapter 21

"Come, let's go swimming."

Seven stood at Bailey's door while she blinked the sleep from her eyes. She was beautiful in her early-morning confusion. Slightly swollen lips, heavy-lidded eyes, her hair a bed-sexy mess. After yesterday's outing at the sculpture garden, he felt an unexpected vulnerability in her presence. She had seen his work and, despite her antiartist sentiments, she hadn't hated him for it. Instead, the outing had brought them closer. Revealed more of themselves to each other.

But even with that, he felt there was some unpleasant thing lurking under her smile.

"What?" Bailey stretched the neck of her sleep shirt to scratch her collarbone.

He held up his swim trunks. "Swimming. Water. Sunshine. Sand."

"Oh." She shoved a hand through her untidy hair and looked back over her shoulder into the room as if she'd misplaced something in there. "When?"

"Now."

She blinked at him again.

"Go ahead and get ready. Mama made us a picnic breakfast so you won't starve."

She muttered something about him loving picnics and disappeared back into the room, closing the door in his face.

"Will you be ready in ten minutes?" he called out to her through the door.

"Half an hour."

When she was finally ready and dressed in pink shorts and a thin white shirt over her bikini, they left the house. As they walked down the steps and through the yard, with the sun burning its particular morning heat over Seven's bare shoulders, chest and back, she seemed to get more alert. More aware.

She turned to him.

"Why aren't you wearing a shirt?"

"Because we're going to the beach, but I packed a shirt in the picnic basket."

She turned her attention back to the path, apparently satisfied with his answer. They walked in companionable silence down the path through the bush and toward the beach. At nine o' clock in the morning, everyone who had to be at work was already there, although the bush sang with the occasional music of voices raised in song, laughter or conversation. Birds chirped from high in the trees. From far off came the sound of a boat's engine as it raced across the water. A nice morning.

Earlier, when he'd woken to the sound of his parents getting ready for work, Seven decided he would take Bailey out. Simon was already long gone back to his house in Kingston and would leave for his job at the university from there. The past two days Seven and Bailey had spent at his parents' house had made him bold. He saw how she interacted with his parents, how she enjoyed their company as much as they enjoyed hers. A good sign. He wanted more. More intimacy, more connectedness. And he knew he could not find that with her in the house. So he had chosen the beach.

"Do you have another woman here?"

"What?" At first, Seven didn't hear her. He had to re-play her words in his head, and when he understood what she'd said, he smiled. She'd said *another* woman. Did that mean she was his main woman? And was that what had been bothering her the day before?

"Are you playing me for a fool?" Bailey asked with the beginnings of agitation in her voice. "Because if you have another woman down here with prior claims on your affec-tions, it doesn't matter how smooth your game is, I'm not having it." Her voice hardened as the words came, raining down on him as her anger grew.

"The only woman I have here is you. And you know that's not quite settled." He paused. "I want you to be my woman. I want to—" He stopped before he said something that would get him slapped.

Bailey's look was pure poison. "I ran into this woman who wanted to kick my butt because she thought I'd sto-len you from her."

"Impossible," he said immediately. "There isn't a woman on this island who can say that I'm her man. No woman in the world, actually."

She looked taken aback by his certainty. "She said your name."

"She's a liar."

"She said the Carmichael boy and…" Her words tapered off.

"She might have been talking about my brother. He is a Carmichael, too, you know." He dared to tease her in the midst of her anger.

"But how can she confuse you two? You look a little bit alike, but with that crazy beard, your brother is unmis-takable."

"Some people must have seen you and me walking down the road that night. They probably thought we were trying to get into something. Or that I was trying to get inside you," he said wryly. "And it was dark. They couldn't tell which twin I was."

Suddenly, he realized something. She was jealous. Seven hid his smile.

"Bailey." He stopped in the middle of the clearing and grasped her shoulders. "There's no one else. I know you saw a woman and she said some things, but I promise that the only woman I want is you."

For a moment, she was silent, carefully watching his face as if to catch him in a lie. Then she stiffened under his hands. "You shouldn't want me," she said. "I'm not the one for you."

"But what if you *are* the one for me?" he asked.

She shook her head, sadness overtaking her face. Seven was startled, realizing she was near to tears. Not Bailey, not his strong Bailey.

"I'm not the one for you," she said.

He wanted her to be wrong. He wanted to prove her wrong. He wanted it with an intensity that surprised him, even with all the things he'd done to get her so far from her home and into his.

"You're for me," he said. His hands tightened around her arms just a fraction, but that movement brought her eyes jerking up to his. "You're for me," he said again, and kissed her.

She didn't turn away from his mouth. She didn't pull back. At first, she did nothing, only allowed him the press of his lips to her lips, his warm hands around her, the early-morning smell of her in his nostrils. Then she kissed him back. Gently, softly. He allowed that gentleness because that was what she wanted. And in that moment, he wanted what she wanted even more than she did.

Her mouth was soft under his, a moist wonder as it

opened for him. His hands slid down her arms and around her waist, pulling her hips into his hips. Her arms twined around his neck and she stretched up to reach to his height and drink more of him. She made a soft sound in her throat, and any gentleness Seven wanted from the kiss threatened to break apart at that passionate sound. She wanted him.

"I don't want you," she whispered against his mouth as she kissed him, pressed her breasts up and into his chest. "I don't."

Seven pulled her closer. His hands felt enormous on her back, over the delicate wings of her shoulder blades, the fragile ladder of her spine. She moaned again in his mouth, and Seven felt his entire body shiver at the sound. His want flooded into him like summer honey. It made him heavy and hot and hard. It made him growl.

She shuddered against him. Her mouth was a moist, hot cavern. Her arms were ropes leading him toward salvation. Once, she had fought this lust like an enemy, butting her head against the attraction they felt for each other, as if to fight would subdue it. But the more she fought, the more he wanted. The more he was convinced she was wrong and he was right.

Bailey raked her fingers along Seven's scalp and lifted her body more into his, as if she wanted to join them then and there in the bright morning. Seven yanked open the picnic basket, grabbed the blanket folded inside it. He swung her up into his arms and pushed into the copse of bushes, by touch alone finding an old path with the trees high and green above them, the ground firm under their feet but littered with leaves, some browning and curled, others damp and smelling of earth, of recent rains.

The lust beat hot and urgently inside him, fed by the sweet press of her mouth against his, her arms on his shoulders, her slim body alongside his. In the deep cover of the woods, she became even bolder, kissed him harder, more firmly, pushed him back against a tree. Seven let go of his control. He opened his mouth hard over hers, kissing her as if the world was ending, as if he'd never kissed her before, as if he'd never get the chance to kiss her again. The blood churned inside his body, boiling temperature, scalding him from head to hips. He burned where she touched him. He wanted to burn some more.

"Seven."

She said his name and nothing else, just the breath of the syllables of his name inside her hot mouth while she kissed him and he kissed her and his body burned to the ground. He pulled her down with him. Hastily spreading the blanket on the hard soil strewn with soft leaves, with the smell of earth and moss and green and life and decay. He took the harshness of the dirt through the thin blanket with his body, holding her above him, cradling her precious weight and allowing gravity and every natural law that disagreed with her reasoning not to be with him to pull her down between his thighs. Her mouth pressed down into his. Legs twining around him, her hands hot against his bare chest. Fingers raking over his nipples.

"Seven," she breathed again in wonder as she touched him.

Whatever control he had shattered. In that moment, she was everything he'd ever wanted, everything he'd ever needed to breathe, to live, just to be. In moments, he rolled them over, reversing their positions so she was the one with her back pressed against the blanket. He fell into the hot junction of her thighs. He was home.

It was his turn to breathe her name. The seat of her femininity welcomed him through her shorts. He felt her heat and wanted nothing more than to tear away that barrier and slide into her, make love with her like he'd dreamed a hundred times since that night on the boat. No, a thousand.

Her hands slid over his chest, a gentle exploration, tentative as if she didn't quite believe where they were, pressed skin to skin. "Seven."

"I want you," he finally said, panting past lips thinned with hunger for her.

His body throbbed with the need to be inside hers. To be hers.

"Then take me," she said.

Seven paused. He forced his mouth away from hers to look down at her. She was breathtaking. Mouth kissed red and even fuller, eyes shining with desire, her quick breath moving the front of her white shirt up and down. Her nipples peaked against the cloth even through the material of her bathing suit. Bailey blinked up at him.

"Are you sure about this?" He forced himself to ask the question, even knowing he'd probably drop dead if she changed her mind and walked away from him.

She licked her wet, kissable lips and lifted her gaze to his. "I want this," she said.

His body sang with her assent. That was all he needed. Seven dove into her mouth like a starving man at a banquet. And she met him, passion for passion, skin for skin, lust for lust. Bailey quickly pulled off her shirt, slid off her bikini top, her shorts and bottoms all before he could get the chance to help. Then she was naked under him, decadently, wantonly nude, with her beautiful brown skin against the blanket, her legs wrapped around him, and the rich and intoxicating smell of her arousal floating up all around them. He was in heaven.

He unzipped himself, quickly shucked off his shorts and swim trunks, eager for her. Bailey clasped his hardness in a loose fist. Stroked him once. Twice.

Seven almost exploded. He fumbled for the condom in his wallet, rolled it on, kissed her harder, pulled her even closer to him and swam into the tightness of her body as if he was made to be there.

She gasped, a deep sound of pleasure, and threw her head back, arched her back, inviting his mouth to her breasts. Seven took her up on the invitation and she gasped again, moving under him in a slow, intense rhythm.

"Yes," she murmured as the wind rose up and brushed over their skin. "Yes!"

Under the sun, with the rays of light burning into his shoulders, back and buttocks, he made love to her. With her legs wrapped tightly around his thighs, the smell of dirt blushing under the sun's heat, her beautiful nakedness and unabashed enjoyment of her body and of his, she made love to him. Pleasure melted the hours away, it rubbed his flesh raw, it shoved an ache into his muscles, made him howl at the sun as she clung to him, her body transported to its own place of delight, the muscles of her throat stretched taut and tight from her gasps and moans of encouragement.

"Seven." She sighed his name in satisfaction.

He shuddered inside her.

When they eventually made it to the beach, Seven didn't want to swim. The taste of her he'd had in the forest made him want her more. He wanted to go back to the house to continue what they'd accomplished twice over in their secluded arbor, but she insisted on going toward their original destination.

"Your mother wouldn't like it if we had sex in her house," Bailey said, backing away from him with a sparkling tease in her eyes.

In that moment, he wanted her even more.

Instead, they dove into the water to cool off, and he

teased her without mercy, touching her and whispering what he wanted to do to her as soon as they left the water, or as soon as they were on their way back to Miami again.

"When is the boat coming back?" she asked, her voice husky and urgent.

"Not soon enough," he growled, sinking his teeth into her damp shoulder.

"Patience is a virtue." She slipped from his embrace and flipped under the water, quick as a fish, and swam away from him toward deeper water. With the jewel-like Caribbean Sea rippling around her, she reached behind her back and undid her bathing suit. Bailey pulled off the flimsy top and threw it toward Seven. It landed near him with a splash, a bright spray of orange in the blue water. "I've never been the virtuous kind."

He grabbed her bathing suit top and swam toward her, pulse heavy with anticipation.

By silent agreement, they spent the rest of the day together. After they left their beach playground, Seven took her for a walk down the long beach away from his parents' house. It was a cliché, Seven found, that women actually enjoyed. But they walked and she didn't do any of the things he'd expected her to do—did not fumble to hold his hand, did not rest her head on his shoulder and sigh at the sun.

Bailey kept her shirt off, like him, hooking her white cotton T-shirt in the back pocket of her shorts, wearing the tiny bikini top that did wonderful things to her already wonderful breasts—full cleavage, curved and eye-catching—that bounced as she walked at his side. And she knew he watched her. That knowledge was in the soft smile that played around her mouth, the way she looked at him, giving him her permission to stare and appreciate what he'd already touched and worshiped with his mouth.

"I'm enjoying this," she said.

"Me, too."

They didn't speak of her reservations about him. He didn't press his suit. In those moments, they were simply two people who'd found themselves on a bright and nearly deserted stretch of beach, with the sun warming their shoulders and desire curling between them like the most delicate and beautiful of snakes.

When they spoke again, it was of other things—what she wanted from her job, what being partner meant to her, why stability was so important for her life and the way she wanted to live it. Seven tentatively told her of his art and the things he sculpted, how many countries had hosted him and purchased his sculptures, what he wanted for his professional life. She didn't interrupt him, only watched his face as he spoke.

"People support the arts more than you realize," he said. "Some of my best clients have been those who needed payment plans. My work is for everyone, not just the very rich."

At a beach bar, little more than a thatched hut on the sand, they stopped with their picnic lunch and bought grapefruit sodas and ate what Seven's mother had prepared for them. The ackee and saltfish sandwiched between thick slices of hard dough bread left them both silent with appreciation, their bare feet hooked on the rungs of the handmade stools as they stared out to sea between the thin poles of the hut frilled with dried coconut-tree leaves.

A breeze trickled through the coconut fronds, a whisper of sound falling into the chorus of waves breaking on the sand, the sound of seagulls. On the water, a dreadlocked man paddled out to sea in a shallow boat bleached pink by the sun.

"I used to dream of being an orphan," she said.

Seven looked away from the quiet ripple of the water.

Bailey shook her head. "It wasn't that I wanted them to die. It never came to my mind as that, not fully. Between all the moving around and times when we would eat canned tuna for days and our parents insisting on taking us everywhere with them, I just wanted to stay in one place. One place. And the only way I knew for that to happen was if my parents weren't around anymore." She picked up her bottle of soda and brought it to her lips, one hand still holding her sandwich. "I never wanted to hurt them. I just wanted them gone from my life."

Seven looked closer and saw tears streaming from her eyes, unacknowledged, as if they were nothing more than liquid light or something incidental to the story she told.

"They wanted to go to the Maldives when we were teenagers. Daddy had a chance at some big fellowship there and the same foundation had some sort of supplementary position for Mama." Bailey took a bite of her sandwich and was silent as she chewed it and swallowed. "I had two more years of high school left, and Bette was about to graduate." Her eyes were far away as if remembering the circumstances of that year, that month, that pivotal week. Seven felt she was building up to something with her story. And it wasn't just guilt about wishing her parents had died so she could have a life of her own.

Seven put the rest of his sandwich on the plate and reached for his soda, giving her his full attention. The bartender talked quietly with a fisherman at the other end of the small bar. Their quiet conversation was as much of a mystery to Seven and Bailey as theirs was to the two men.

"They wanted to take us with them. Neither of us had been to that part of the world before. My sister was interested, but I was done pulling up my life to follow them to the ends of the earth. I told them no. I begged Bette to stay with me. At first she ignored me, but I pleaded with her until she agreed. She would stay in America and go to college and I'd finish high school and follow her to college. By then, we were old enough to take care of ourselves. Bette was eighteen and we both had jobs."

Her hand began to shake as she spoke. Seven took her sandwich and put it on the plate. She absently wiped her hands on a napkin and sipped from the green bottle. Then she continued the story of her parents reluctantly leaving their two young daughters in Miami and taking a boat to their next destination.

"The boat was hijacked by pirates, can you believe that?" Bailey shook her head, lips pulled in a grimace that she may have thought was a smile. "That sort of craziness could only happen to them. Who gets killed by pirates in the twenty-first century?"

The tears ran faster down her face, trickling into her mouth and down her chin to hit the counter of the little outdoor bar. Her tears darkened the wood in small, random circles.

"You didn't kill them, Bailey."

"I know I didn't force them to go out to sea, but I know the power of my mind. I was done with moving around, really done. And then they were gone." She put down her bottle of soda. "When I look at you, I remember them in a way I haven't done in years. When I'm with you, I feel them." She put a hand to her face and pulled it back, looking surprised to see that it came away wet. "I miss them."

"There's nothing wrong with that. Just like there's nothing wrong with the kind of life you've chosen for yourself."

"Of course you would say that. You're just too damn perfect, you know that?" She squinted up at him as if his alleged perfection was an affront to her.

Seven smiled, then reached across the small space for her hand. "I'm far from perfect, but I do know that I like you. It may mean nothing in the bigger scheme of your life, but I want you to give this a chance to make us both happy. The past is past. Give the future the opportunity to be better than you think it's going to be."

She shook her head, releasing a bittersweet smile. "You damn optimist."

He smiled. "Not really. I just want to get into your shorts again, and the best chance for that to happen is when you're happy or even laughing at me."

That surprised a laugh from her.

"See?"

She shoved playfully at his shoulder. "You are ridiculous."

"If that's what you want, I'll be a ridiculous optimist for you."

Her delicate smile slowly disappeared until it was just her deep brown eyes staring into his, the tears drying on her face and the warm weight of her hands in his hands.

"Can I get you two something else?" The bartender's appearance broke the spell between them.

Seven slowly released Bailey's hands and braced his forearms against the bar. He flicked a look at the bartender before glancing once again at Bailey, assessing her willingness to extend their day. Bailey nodded and reached for the rest of her sandwich.

"Yes, man," he said to the bartender. "A couple of Red Stripes."

On a whim, he decided to check himself and Bailey into one of the seaside guest houses at Sea Vista Cottages and Resorts. After the beer and conversation at the small beach hut, Seven realized that Bailey needed more. *He* needed more. So, he left their picnic basket on the beach and flagged down a taxi man to take them to the nearby resort.

As they picked up the keys from the front desk of the main cottage at Sea Vista, Bailey frowned at him.

"In case you didn't realize it, I don't have any change of clothes," she said.

But she was looking around the spacious cottage with definite interest. Taking note of the multicultural collection of tourists walking through the lobby, the wide-open windows with a view of the sea on one side and the mountains on the other.

"You don't need any clothes," he said.

"Oh, really?"

The red-suited porter walked them out of the reception cottage at the front of the sprawling property and out the front door to the cement walkway bisecting a long stretch of impressively manicured grass. Their destination was the small guest cottage tucked into the cove at the far end of the property. Seven had stayed there before. He and Bailey followed the red-clad back of the thin older man, who obviously took pride in the uniform he wore, strutting down the walk as proudly as the peacocks parading on the resort grounds.

After unlocking the door of the pale blue cottage at the end of a path lined with seashells, the porter handed Seven the keys.

"Meals are available all day. As is service of any kind that you may need. Simply call the office and all will be provided for you."

"You've been very helpful." Seven reached into his pocket for a hundred-dollar bill. "Thank you."

The porter discreetly slipped the money into his jacket pocket. He clasped his hands behind his back and nodded to them both. "Enjoy your stay at Sea Vista."

Then he turned and began making his way back toward

the main cottage. Bailey looked after him with an amused expression.

"Do you think if we asked for two naked girls dipped in white chocolate we'd get them?"

"Probably. This *is* a full-service resort, after all."

Bailey glanced at him, perhaps wondering if he'd asked for—and received—something similar in the past. Seven quirked an eyebrow, then gestured for her to precede him into the cottage. After the tiniest pause and a narrow-eyed look, she stepped through the white doorway.

As she walked past him, Seven dropped his eyes to her curvaceous backside swishing in the pale shorts. He swallowed heavily, remembering the feel of that soft flesh in his hands as they had made love under the trees, and the way she shuddered in his arms as she achieved her satisfaction. He turned away to close the front door, gripping the doorknob in his hand and firmly seating the heavy white door in the threshold. Seven took a deep breath to get his libido under control.

"You're being a tad presumptuous, aren't you?" she asked.

Seven turned around. Behind Bailey, the French doors of the living room allowed in a view of a tall breadfruit tree and the rainbow-colored hammocks strung underneath it. Beyond the tree lay the pool and a pair of deck chairs facing the sea. The sky was a soft and seductive blue. The perfect frame for her luscious figure, the tempting pink of her mouth.

"How so?"

"You're assuming that I'll sleep with you here."

"I didn't bring you here for sex," Seven said, although he had hoped their mutual desires would take their natural course. "This is a chance for you to relax and enjoy another side of Jamaica."

He tossed the keys to the cottage on the coffee table and reached up to pull off his shirt, gratified when her eyes widened and fastened on his bared skin.

Seven grinned. "I always come here to see my family, but make sure I enjoy Jamaica as a tourist, too. It's a sensual experience." He tossed his shirt on the couch. "Come outside with me."

She hesitated, eyes still on his body, her stance clearly ambivalent about what she wanted to happen. Wanting him, but battling against the emotion. The desire like a noose around her neck. Seven didn't want her ambivalent. He wanted her to want him as much as he longed for her. And he wasn't going to take for granted that she'd afford him the same privileges to her body that he'd had that morning. His desire for her was wide, deep and all-encompassing. But he wasn't about to convince or coerce her into sleeping with him again.

He walked past her to open the French doors, letting in the salt-sweet air, the sound of the sea. Outside, he drew in a deep lungful of air, looking out at the turquoise water, the sailboats coasting across the rippling surface. He left the deck and pool behind, walking across the grass and down the hill.

"Where are we going?"

Bailey appeared at his side in her bikini. T-shirt and shorts gone, eyes filled with curiosity...and humor.

She had made a joke of it, whatever she had been feeling inside the cottage. Now she stood at his side with her smiling mouth and her body bared for his appreciation and perhaps for her own comfort, as well.

"We're going to play with dolphins, hopefully." He smiled down at her, pushing his desire behind him, focusing on her warm and lovely presence close to him.

She chuckled. "I can't believe you actually told me where we're going."

"Well, I can't be mysterious and cryptic all the time. That would be too predictable." He started walking and she fell in step beside him.

The hill sloped down to a cliff, a gentle decline down to the beach and the sharp blue water, with foamy waves and flocks of seabirds floating over them.

"This is so incredible!"

Bailey gripped Seven's waist as she looked over the edge to the sea, the beach below. "If I lived here I'd be in a constant state of awe. This island is so beautiful."

"I am in a state of awe. But I'm the man—I have to be cool about things like that." He grinned down at her.

"Miami is beautiful, but that's nothing compared to this. Not to mention it's warm all the time. None of that winter chill to deal with. Paradise all the time."

"I come here as often as I can. Sometimes, I have dreams about being like Simon and buying a house where I was born and having a family and being one of those successful Jamaicans who actually live in Jamaica."

"But then you wake up?"

"Yes," Seven said. "Dreams are dreams for a reason."

"It would be amazing to live here." She took in a deep breath and turned in a complete circle, arms spread wide.

"But what about your partnership at the firm?"

At the closed look that descended on Bailey's face, Seven was immediately sorry that he'd mentioned her job. She frowned, looked away from him, back to the soaring sky and the blue sea.

Idiot.

Shaking his head at himself, he put a hand at the small of her back and guided her down the hill, their sandaled feet sliding over the limestone rock and sparse grass. At the end of the slope, the hill curved, and the land flattened. And just a few feet away, a hidden corner of the sea appeared; jewel green and shallow, a man-made semicircle of rocks created a cove perfect for swimming. The sand was almost blinding in its whiteness.

"Are you joking?" Bailey stared. "How much more beautiful can this place get?"

Seven grabbed her up into his arms, and she squealed.

"What are you doing!"

He ran a few yards, her slight weight hot and squirming against him, then tossed her into the water.

"Seven!"

She screamed his name as she hit the water, her limbs flailing. He jumped in with her, water splashing up into his face. Beside him, through the sting of the salt water, he saw Bailey laughing, her body already righting itself in the water, swimming toward him with vengeance in her face.

"Not fair!" she cried out as she leaped on top of him in the water, sinking him below the surface.

He held on to her body, senses open to take all of her in, the feel of her body under the water, the sadness falling away from her face as they wrestled like puppies.

"I can't believe you did that!" She coughed, swimming back as he came for her.

"No serious faces allowed," he said, and tugged her foot.

She ducked under the water, twisted and came up in a spout of water to pull him under. Dimly, Seven heard a faint chirping sound, felt a nudge against his thigh.

"Oh!"

Bailey suddenly released him, her face encased in wonder. She swam back from him, her arms moving lazily in the water as she looked at something just beyond him. Seven turned to look. A dolphin. It chirped, splashing close to him, pressed its face to his before darting back in the water.

"Oh, my God! You just kissed a dolphin!"

"I think it just kissed me," he said drily. But he smiled at the joyous look on her face.

She swam toward the dolphin, her movements gentle in the water. "Hey, baby," she crooned softly. "Hey."

Something moved inside Seven, wondering what it would be like if she ever talked to him like that. Looking forward to that day if it should ever come. Then he pushed aside the thought, swam from the sea creature and allowed Bailey to come closer to it. The dolphin chirped again, almost teasing her as Seven swam away. Something hard thumped him in the back and he turned, ending up nose to chest with a second dolphin. It was quiet, only smiling at him, or at least baring its little dolphin teeth while Bailey swam toward the other creature in search of a kiss of her own.

"I want a kiss," Bailey said softly. "Can you kiss me, too?"

As she came closer to the dolphin, it chirped again, swimming backward away from her, playing with her. Bailey laughed. She spun in the water. "He's so cute! Did you see that?"

At the sight of the second dolphin near Seven, her mouth fell open again. "What are you, the dolphin whisperer?"

"Maybe they like my cologne."

She pouted. "All I wanted was a kiss."

Seven laughed at her crestfallen expression. When she looked even more disappointed, he swam closer to her, still chuckling. "I can give you a kiss," he said.

Before he could change his mind, Seven closed the small space between them, water splashing, to slip his arms around her and kiss her unprotesting mouth. She sighed, slid her arms up and around his neck, kissed him in return.

He had only meant it to be a tease, but with the pressure of her lips, the familiar pleasure blossomed. Her tongue slid in his mouth, her slippery body moved against his, then the kiss became serious. Hot.

Bailey made a soft noise against his mouth, sliding even closer to him, her body twisting against his until his desire rose hard and insistent between them. Something bumped his shoulder. A chirp. Then a long nose shoved between them. Bailey laughed, leaned in to peck the dolphin on the nose, her arms still hanging around Seven's neck.

"I've never had a threesome quite like this one," he said.

"Me, either," she said, tossing him a wink.

Had she just said what he thought she'd said? "Wait a minute…!"

The dolphin gave another chirp and glided away to join his mate.

Bailey laughed and chased after the dolphin, her long legs splashing in the water. But the dolphins were faster, quickly turning in the water, chirping at her before escaping the cove for the larger sea. Laughing, Bailey waved at them until they dove into the water and out of sight.

She turned quickly, splashing up crystalline drops of seawater that landed on her shoulders, making her glisten in the sun as if kissed by diamonds.

"That was pretty damn amazing. I've done a lot in my life, but I have to say that's the first time for dolphin swimming." Her smile was the most beautiful thing Seven had seen in a long time.

"They come to this cove all the time. I brought you here on the off chance of a sighting." He grinned. "I see you're pleased."

"I'm more than pleased." She swam close to him, kissed

him very lightly on the lips. "Thank you. Today has been perfect."

He settled his hands on her hips. "Don't thank me yet. The day is far from over."

Her smile widened. "Have I ever told you how wonderful you are?"

"Hmm. I should show you dolphins more often."

She giggled and swam away.

They lazed in the cove for another hour, enjoying the sun and the warm water, Bailey floating on top of the turquoise miracle, her slender body tempting beyond all imagining. But Seven didn't touch her again. He simply enjoyed the sight of her, her lithe body, the happiness in her eyes, the way she touched him spontaneously, unselfconsciously. Yes, maybe he should show her dolphins more often.

When she grew tired, Seven drew her from the water and took her back up the hill to the hammock just outside their cottage. Skin warm and bathing suit dripping wet, she lay in the hammock under the breadfruit tree, looking up at him as if he hung the moon. Then her eyes slid shut.

While she napped, he lay in the hammock next to hers, relishing the heat of the sun on his naked chest, the sight of her next to him. Although he knew he shouldn't get used to her company—she hated artists, and she hated that she wanted him—he felt even more drawn to her. Even more helpless to his attraction for her. He was officially whipped.

Chapter 22

Night brought them back to his parents' house. They slipped inside the door after nine o'clock, silently, the hush of a well-spent day around them. Inside the house, Bailey automatically stepped away from Seven, not wanting to insult his mother with any display of intimacy.

The day with Seven had been an awakening. Restful and sensual. After she'd woken up from her nap in the hammock, she and Seven had soaked in the Jacuzzi, then ordered a lavish lobster-and-shrimp dinner, which they'd eaten by the pool while watching the sunset. After dinner, they'd had drinks in the main bar of the resort, then enjoyed a swim in the unnecessarily heated pool before checking out and making their way back to the Carmichaels' house.

Bailey had completely enjoyed herself. Normally—other than the time she spent with Bette—every interaction required some extra effort, needed her to be something more than what she was. Seven asked her for nothing but herself. And she loved it.

She didn't want to, of course, but no matter how much she'd fought for them, her wants had rarely coincided with her reality.

The house was dark as they made their way inside. A slice of light under the room down the hall from hers—

Simon's room—was the only indication someone else was in the house.

Seven brushed past her, deliberately, she thought, bringing his masculine scent to her nose. He had put his shirt on, but was no less magnificent, no less tempting. His teeth flashed at her in the dark.

"Go ahead and shower first," he murmured as they stood outside her door. He leaned down to her, nearly whispering the words. His breath brushed her mouth.

She deliberately breathed him in.

"Why are you whispering?" she asked, keeping close to him a few moments longer. They couldn't go into the shower together, and he couldn't follow her into the bedroom. Her skin tingled with the desire to do both these things. And then...

"I don't want to wake Simon up," Seven whispered.

"Okay." She stepped closer to him, sipping more of his breath. The warmth of his skin radiated through his white T-shirt and shorts. If she wanted to, she could touch him. Bailey licked her lips. "I'm going to take a shower."

His eyes devoured her body. "Okay."

The bedroom door down the hall creaked open and the strip of light widened, spilled across the pale tile floors.

"What are you two doing out here?" Simon didn't whisper.

Bailey stepped back away from Seven, her fingers curling in disappointment. "Talking," she said. Or at least that was what she'd meant to say. Simon flipped on the hallway light to get a better look at them, but it was Bailey who got a better look at him. His feet were bare. A pale checked pair of pajama pants hung from his lean hips, emphasizing the subtle musculature of his belly and chest. He didn't have his glasses on. He'd gotten a haircut. And he had shaved.

"Feeling civilized again, brother?" Seven asked. He

shoved his hands in the pocket of his shorts and leaned back against the wall while all Bailey could do was stare from one brother to the other.

"You're *identical* twins?"

"But I'm the better-looking one," Simon offered from under the warm glow of the hall light.

And still Bailey stared. Their faces were absolutely alike in every way, down to the wicked arch of eyebrow Simon leveled on her as he took in her astonishment. She searched for differences. Simon's body was lean and finely muscled, while Seven was hard and thick—hills of pectorals, deltoids and a flat belly she could do a whole load of laundry on.

"I didn't think the beard and glasses concealed that much," he said.

"They do."

Seven gave his brother a dismissive glance. "I think your woman's on the loose again."

"What are you talking about?"

"Winsome threatened Bailey. Somebody saw me with Bailey last night and thought I was you, messing around on Winsome."

Simon turned to Bailey. It was disconcerting, like watching an image walk out of a mirror and into the world with its original.

"You okay? Winsome didn't do anything to you, did she?"

"The fact that you have to ask that question, brother, is seriously disturbing." Seven shook his head. "Winsome needs to be committed."

Simon sucked his teeth. "I'm sure she was just playing around."

"Either Winsome is a psycho, or she's very misunderstood. You can't have it both ways, Simon."

His brother made another dismissive noise.

Bailey shook her head. "I'm going to take a shower," she said.

"My brother would love to come in there with you, but Mama would castrate him if he tried."

Seven winced. "I don't need that."

"Me, either," Bailey murmured.

She felt the boys' eyes on her back as she turned away and ducked into the bedroom. As soon as she closed the door, she heard them start talking quickly in patois, something she didn't even try to follow as she took off her clothes, put on the robe and grabbed her towel and toothbrush. When she went back into the hallway to find the bathroom, they were gone, the deep rumble of their voices coming from beyond the living room. Probably on the porch.

Bailey stepped into the bathroom and closed the door behind her. Turned the shower on and stepped under the room-temperature spray. Water rushed down her head and face, gushing pleasantly down her chest, swirling along her skin, along the places Seven had touched and kissed. She leaned back against the pale tile of the shower and allowed the water to pour over her.

Identical twins. She almost couldn't believe it. When she'd met Seven, she thought him unique in all the world. Beautiful and seductive, like an incubus from her dreams. And in Jamaica, she'd found another one of him. But aside from his face, Simon was nothing like Seven. The body he wore under his ratty clothes proved it—a runner's body, while Seven's seemed sculpted by work, by the gods themselves.

Under the cool water, she felt her own body beginning to heat as she remembered the feel of Seven against her, over her, as he'd made love to her on the ground, then in the water as she'd climbed all over him, sliding over his slick musculature, which was her perfect playground. Maybe it was time to think about something else.

Bailey swallowed and reached for the soap.

After her shower she went to find the brothers on the porch. They sprawled on opposite ends of the dimly lit area, talking softly. As she walked out into the night with them, Seven stirred.

"You smell nice," he said.

His brother laughed. "You're trying too hard to get into her panties, brother."

Bailey settled a look on him. "He doesn't have to try to get where I want him to be."

Even in the intimate darkness, she could see the astonishment on his face. She chuckled. "What are you, five years old?"

Simon recovered quickly enough. "Five is too young to enjoy the pleasures I've grown accustomed to," he said.

"Everything isn't about sex, Simon." Seven leaned back in his chair, moved his head only slightly to look at his brother.

"True, not everything, but most things are. It's the great equalizer, brother. Everyone has sex sometime or other."

"I don't even know why I'm having this conversation with you." Seven laughed, half in exasperation, half in amusement.

Before he could say another word, a clatter of high heels sounded against the porch steps. A lightning movement that in a moment revealed the woman Bailey had seen on the street the other morning. She looked very different from the wild, mad woman who'd wanted to fight her. She had cleaned herself up, wore high heels and a tight-fitting orange dress revealing an abundant spill of cleavage, and her long, permed hair was pulled up to the top of her head in some sort of elaborate French roll. She looked as though she was out on a date.

"You bastard, Simon!" she screamed. "I knew you were just like all the others. You just couldn't wait to go out and find some foreign slut." Her narrow-eyed gaze focused on Simon, who had half risen up in his chair at her sudden appearance. A hand rested on the arm of his chair, but he still sat and watched her with a stunned look on his face.

"You two-timing, dirty, good-for-nothing, patronizing, wannabe-Mother-Teresa ass! I should have never let you take me home that night. So what if you're good in bed. I can have that anytime I want. Anytime!" Before Simon could say anything, the woman spun to face Bailey. "You man-stealing bitch!" She flew at Bailey.

Simon catapulted from his chair just as Bailey shot to her feet, ready to meet the oncoming woman. He grabbed her around the waist and jerked her against him. She screamed more angry words at Bailey, flailed in his arms. But Bailey couldn't help but notice Winsome did not hit him. For all the motion of her elbows and legs, the sharp flash of her high heels that could have easily jabbed between his legs or even in his thigh, she took care not to hurt him. It was Bailey she wanted to damage.

"Hello, Winsome."

Seven said the words softly, casually from his partially hidden place on the porch, but Bailey had the sudden impression of a coiling, a readiness.

The woman looked at him and seemed to deflate. Her flailing arms stopped, and the flow of poison from her mouth stuttered to a halt. "Oh. I didn't know you were home," she said.

"Now you know."

"Oh." The woman looked from Seven's lazy slouch to Bailey, who sat near him, and seemed to put things together in her mind. She bit her lip. Then twisted in Simon's grip, hands grasping the ropy arms that held her. "You should have told me he was here!"

Simon shook his head. He seemed stunned still at the night's events, but not angry, as though he approved of her madness in confronting some imaginary rival for his affections.

"We need to talk," he said without putting her down.

"I'm not here to talk!" she shouted at him.

"That's obvious." He gave a thorough glance at her outfit, the beautifully styled hair and long, glittering earrings. He looked at Bailey, then at Seven. "Excuse me," he said, then picked up the woman more fully in his arms and carried her off the porch to the soundtrack of her outraged screams.

Bailey tracked their passage through the night by sound, the woman's heavy breathing, her shouts. They struggled together down the steps, down the hill and beyond the front gates of the yard. Then the sounds abruptly died.

Bailey released the tense breath she hadn't realized she had been holding. She sat back in her chair, blinking into the darkness.

"Thank God your parents weren't here to see that."

Seven made a noise of impatience. "She probably planned it that way. I'm sure Simon told her this is my parents' date night. They're in Ochi until tomorrow morning."

"Tomorrow morning?"

"Yes."

Bailey thought, suddenly, of what that meant for her. What that meant for Seven. Except for Simon's indifferent presence, they would be alone in the house. They could do…whatever they wanted. Their gazes collided. Bailey swallowed. The space separating them on the porch seemed to narrow. It would take nothing for her to stand up and cross the small half-dark space to him, to slip into his lap and kiss him, unbutton his shirt, fill her hands with the feel of him. She swallowed again.

In moments, Seven was standing at her chair, his eyes filled with want. He dropped to his knees in front of her. Before he could come any closer, she pressed her hands against his chest, trying to hold him off. He was hot and hard under her palm.

"Your brother will be back here any second," she murmured, already drowning in his hungry gaze.

"No, he won't." Seven's voice was a deep growl. "He and Winsome are at her house by now. Or in the bushes."

Bailey's eyes flickered closed at the unrelenting heat of him so close. She wanted to protest against what they both wanted to do, but couldn't find the words. Seven's fingers sank into her skin. He brought his mouth close and kissed her. A shock of desire ran through Bailey, a tingling, a hard fist of longing that jerked in her stomach. She moaned against his mouth and returned his urgent kiss. He clasped her thighs, her back, and lifted her high against him as he stood. Not breaking the kiss, he carried her through the front door, down the hall and into his room. Her room.

He kicked the door shut behind them and dropped her on the bed, following bare seconds later with the heaviness of his body. He felt so right against her. As if he was made for her. For this moment.

"We can't," she said, although her body clamored for what only he could give.

Her legs were liquid for him, her center molten in readiness for his touch. He pulled down the straps of her dress, kissing her shoulders, hands under her skirt, over her bare thighs. She opened up for him, and her head swayed back to give him access to her throat. Desire rushed through her. Only for him.

"We can't," she murmured, gasping. "Your parents."

They had promised not to disrespect the house. They weren't married; it wasn't right. But his mouth latched on to her breast and she lost her senses. He slid a hand between her thighs, and she sighed, then gasped at the delicate intrusion, his knowing touch on the center of her passion.

Seven touched her, his mouth moving like hot silk over her skin, his fingers moving between her thighs, delicately, then insistently. A tightness pulled hard in her womb. The fullness in her grew larger and larger. She moved against the bed, under Seven, a hot burn of sweat under her dress as Seven touched her, pulled her higher.

"Seven…" She gripped his shoulder, bit into the skin through his shirt.

Bailey clenched her eyes tightly as her body responded to him, the molten heat of her desire flowing from her, Seven catching it in his palm, caressing her, loving her. "Oh, God!" She clutched him tighter and tighter. Her bare heels pushed down into the bed. Her thighs flowered wider for him.

"Seven!"

A burning flush overwhelmed her body. Her world exploded. Bright, hot colors danced behind her tightly clenched eyelids. Bailey panted, her heart thumping, fingers grasping in his shirt, the riot of her flesh slowly calming.

For a moment, all she could do was lie under him, gasping, the aftershocks tripping through her body while Seven's heavy weight hovered over her. He sat up. His dark gaze blazed with unfulfilled passion. But he pushed away from her even more, not hiding the evidence of his lust for her. He put the two fingers damp from her flesh to his lips, licked them, watching her, his beautiful lips faintly flushed red.

"Think about this when you're sleeping in my bed tonight," he said roughly. "I know I will."

Then he stood up from the bed and left the room.

Bailey blinked after him, wishing. Still wanting.

Chapter 23

Early morning came with a friendly face, the sound of Mrs. Millicent knocking on her door.

"Are you awake, dear?"

Bailey wasn't really, but struggled up from the bedclothes tossed by her restless Seven-deprived sleep and went to answer the knock. The sky outside her window blushed with the first signs of sunrise, and birdsong warbled at her. A cock crowed in the distance.

"Good morning." She greeted her lover's mother with a genuine smile. In the past few days, the woman had made Bailey feel more welcome than she had any right to.

"Good morning, dear. You should dress and come into the kitchen."

Puzzled, Bailey nodded. After Mrs. Millicent left, she washed her face, brushed her teeth and pulled on one of her sister's dresses. Mrs. Millicent waited for her at the small dining table tucked away in the kitchen, drinking from a mug of what looked like hot chocolate.

The kitchen door leading out to their yard was open to let in the crisp smell of morning. Like the front yard, the back was a riot of growing things, a carefully manicured chaos of fruit trees and vegetation she didn't recognize but somehow sensed were edible. A pale dog strolled past the open door without so much as a glance in their direction.

"Do you take coffee, tea or chocolate?"

"Uh, whatever you're having is fine." She didn't want her to go through any effort to make something just for her. Bailey sat down at the table while her hostess fired up the stove under a small saucepan already containing hot chocolate. By the time she took a cup and saucer down from the cupboard, rinsed them and cut four slices of hard dough bread from a thick slab on the counter, the hot chocolate was ready. She poured some for Bailey and brought it back to the table along with the bread.

"My husband is the cook of the family, but he's resting now, God bless him." She settled into the chair opposite Bailey with a sigh.

"Seven told me what a great cook he is," Bailey offered. "But said your baking is out of this world."

Mrs. Millicent smiled at the compliment. "It's good to be appreciated," she said. "Especially by people you love."

"Yes, it is."

Mrs. Millicent took a drink from her cup of hot chocolate, which already had bits of bread floating in it. She dipped a slice of bread in the cup and lustily bit into it. She didn't seem in any hurry to talk, simply content to sip her chocolate, eat the chocolate-dipped bread and share the early-morning quiet. Bailey relaxed into her chair, savoring the sweet smell of the new day.

"You know, Seven has one favorite dish that only I make for him." Mrs. Millicent's look was inviting, conspiratorial. "Do you want to know what it is?"

"Of course." Bailey couldn't resist her invitation. This was where Seven got so much of his appeal from.

"Finish your chocolate and bread and I'll show you."

They finished their light meal, talking about this and that, nothing important, how Bailey enjoyed the island, if she'd ever been there before, would she ever come back.

They washed up the cups and saucers and put them in the dish rack to dry, then Mrs. Millicent pulled from the top of the fridge a bowl full of ingredients—an onion, big cloves of garlic, sprigs of thyme, a bright orange pepper and a brown coconut, still in its hard shell. The bowl was large and old, nearly the size of the dish rack and made from a deep, dark wood with swirls of alternating dark and pale lines. It looked old, the outside darkened and tempered by years of handling.

"This is beautiful!" Bailey said, reaching out to touch the bowl. "What's it made from?"

Mrs. Millicent looked pleased that she'd asked, as if Bailey had just passed some sort of test.

"My grandmother gave me this bowl the day I got married. She said as long as I used this to make food for my man and my family, our love will remain strong like the wood." She touched the bowl, almost reverently. "It's the strongest wood in the world, lignum vitae."

"That's the national flower of Jamaica, isn't it?"

Mrs. Millicent looked at her slyly. "How you know that?"

Bailey found herself blushing. After she met Seven and couldn't get him out of her mind, she had done a Google search on him, looked up everything about Jamaica just because he was born there. "Research," she said, looking down at the bowl. Mrs. Millicent laughed.

"Never mind that, dear. Let me show you what will bring my son to his knees for you." She looked at Bailey again. "Aside from the obvious, that is."

"Mrs. Millicent!"

Seven's mother laughed again.

They worked side by side in the kitchen, with Bailey cutting up the onion, garlic and thyme while Mrs. Millicent cracked open the coconut, discarded the shell and broke up the hard pieces of meat.

"The old-time way is to use a grater, but I always end up scraping up my knuckles."

Mrs. Millicent brought out a blender and dropped the pieces of coconut in it then set the old-fashioned machine on Grate. By the time the sun rose fully and the morning was Technicolor bright, the milk had been separated from the coconut and was simmering in a pot, boiled down to its essence with the onion, garlic, thyme, salt and pepper. Bailey heard sounds of the men stirring in the bedrooms down the hall.

"Now for the crab and shrimp." Mrs. Millicent pointed to the fridge.

Bailey retrieved a white bowl of shrimp and separated crab meat and turned to give it to her. She almost tripped over her own two feet. Seven stood in the doorway, shirtless and wearing a pair of dark pajamas, similar to the ones his brother had had on last night. They hung off his hips, too, but where Simon's look had been attractive enough, Seven was breathtaking. Heart-stopping.

"Give me the bowl, child." Mrs. Millicent's voice was ripe with amusement.

Bailey hastily passed the shrimp and crab mixture to her.

"I smell run dung," Seven said, rubbing his flat belly. "Are you trying to make me stay longer, Mama? You know we leave today."

Today? Bailey looked briefly at him, then away. In the small kitchen, his presence was an intoxicant. His sleep smell reached out to her through the rich and sweet aroma of the coconut. Suddenly, she ached to sleep with him, to know what it was like to be with him first thing in the morning, to kiss his sleep-sour mouth and mess the sheets again with their morning lovemaking. Bailey cleared her throat and backed away. He came farther into the small kitchen.

"I'm teaching Bailey how to make it so you don't have to come home next time complaining how you haven't had a decent meal in however long." Mrs. Millicent poured the meat into the pot and covered it. Stirred it. "Don't worry, you'll have plenty to take with you on the way back to Miami."

"Thank you, Mama. You're an angel."

"Don't thank me. This other angel here said she wanted to learn."

A wide smile split Seven's face. He moved closer to Bailey. "Good morning," he murmured.

"Good morning." She looked into his face fully for the first time that morning.

A soft puff of surprised breath left her mouth. She felt herself smiling up at him like a fool. Even after all this time, Seven was as beautiful to her as the newly risen sun, and that thought filled her with delight.

Chapter 24

The boat left Jamaica for Miami in the late afternoon. As the *Dirty Diana* pulled away from shore, Seven stood on the deck with Bailey and waved to his family as the sun burned all around them, illuminating their beautiful, sad smiles. They watched the dock become smaller, along with the forms of his family who waved and shouted goodbyes.

Bailey stood next to him, wearing one of his new favorites, the white lace dress that fluttered loosely around her body, the perfect backdrop to her dark brown skin. With only inches between them, it seemed only right to settle his arm around her shoulders. She leaned into him, still watching the small brown dots on the sand.

"How often do you see them?" she asked.

"Not often enough."

She sighed. "They're wonderful people. You're very lucky."

"I know."

When his family had disappeared and only a low blue line of horizon remained of where they had once stood, by silent agreement the two of them found the long lounging chairs under a shady overhang on the boat and sat together. The wind whipped through Bailey's hair, pushed the fabric of the dress even closer to her body. She was everything wonderful he'd ever seen.

The chair creaked as Seven sank into it at her side. It was another beautiful day on the sea, a paradise of turquoise water, blue sky and the occasional passage of other boats heading to destinations unknown. The *Dirty Diana*'s engine growled as she made her stately way across the water, taking them back to Miami, where it had all begun.

"This could just be about now," he said.

She didn't pretend to misunderstand him. She only nodded.

"I know I'm not the kind of man you want, so let this be about this trip, this place. Once we get to Miami, we can go our separate ways. I won't pressure you for more."

Bailey pressed her lips together, her eyes squinting as she looked out to the vast blue emptiness. "You're not what I expected," she said.

"What does that mean?"

Her eyes found his. "Nothing. I guess it means nothing."

Something weighed heavily on her—he could tell. But whatever it was, she wasn't ready to share it. Her lips were shut to him. She stood up and held out her hand.

"Come, let's enjoy the rest of our time together."

He looked at her, feeling the surprise settle into his spine, the awareness of what she meant, the curved sweetness of her body above him framed by the bright sky.

Chapter 25

She couldn't let him go. She thought about it and she couldn't do it. It was stupid, she knew that. It was a gamble against her future, but the sweetness he'd shown her on the boat, even before they left, and the magic in his touch had convinced her, had turned her against herself.

Bailey led him downstairs to her quarters, pulled off his clothes, then hers, and made love with him in that bed for the second time. It was everything it had been that first time—surprise, pleasure, intensity, perfection—and more.

Seven beside her was large and tender, and inside her he was a miracle of sensation, a slow building of lust and pleasure until the fire consumed them, sweat drenched them. His muscular body settled down onto hers, moved over and into her, his muscles clenching and unclenching, his hot breath chuffing against her neck, her nails digging into his back until they found that crying-out place together. Again and again.

The next few days were like a honeymoon. Or what she imagined one to be like. Sex at least six times in a day and meals taken together in bed, whispered intimacies deep into the night and the fulfillment of a fantasy she'd had earlier at his parents' house—waking to his hands on her body, his mouth on her tender places, early-morning orgasms and shared laughter. It was perfect and she couldn't let him go.

* * *

They arrived in Miami on a Sunday. Seven woke at Bailey's side with a smile on his face. They had fallen asleep in a tangle of arms and legs on the deck of the boat after making love under the thin protection of a sheet constantly threatening to blow away in the brisk breeze. The air smelled different, with hints of the city—exhaust, money, people stacked on top of each other.

He felt good. His body ached pleasantly from days of constant lovemaking, and the smell of her lay around him like a soft cloud. He was happy. Then he remembered. It was his last day with her.

His smile shriveled.

Beside him, she stirred and moaned softly. "Did we stop?"

"Not yet. We slowed down, though." He let the news leak reluctantly from him. "We're almost there."

She must have heard something in his voice, a reluctance, maybe even a sadness. She sat up and the sheets pooled around her waist. He pulled them back to her breasts with the slightest of smiles. "People," he said.

She looked around as if noticing the other boats for the first time, over a dozen of them sailing through Biscayne Bay. Bailey shrugged, smiling. But she kept the sheet up to her chest.

"What's wrong?" she asked.

"Nothing for you," he said with a rueful smile.

"What do you mean?"

"It's back to the real world and the real men you'd invite into your life. Now that we're back here, I step out."

She bit her lip, leaned away from him. The wind played in her hair, tossing it like a dark banner around her face, spider-webbing over her eyes as she watched him.

"I—" She didn't continue. She cleared her throat. "I need to put some clothes on for this," she muttered.

"For what?" His gut clenched. "Just tell me whatever it is you have to say. Tell me now." Seven could feel himself growing angry at the situation, a mechanism to push aside the sadness that was eating him alive. But he couldn't blame her. She had told him what she wanted and didn't want from the very beginning. He'd thought he could change her. That was his fault. His anger fell away. "Tell me," he said.

Bailey swallowed and reached out to him. Her fingers settled very gently on his chest. It was a small torture. The last time she had touched him like that, he was inside her, their breaths as one, and she'd looked up at him as if there was no one else in the world for her. Seven flinched from her.

She looked at him with hurt eyes, then her gaze flickered away. She seemed to understand, because she met his eyes again, determined to say whatever was on her mind.

"If there's one thing this past week has taught me, it's that there are no certainties in life," Bailey said. "The things you expect sometimes never materialize. People aren't always who you expect them to be." She paused, carefully watching his face. "I want us to try."

Something in his chest leaped, but he clenched his teeth, unwilling to jump to any conclusions.

"What do you mean?"

She laughed ruefully. "You're not going to make this easy for me, are you?" Without waiting for an answer, she pressed close to him, dropping the sheet, and melded her chest to his. "Will you be my boyfriend, Seven Carmichael?"

He chuckled, feeling the heaviness of the past few minutes fall away from him. "I don't know. It depends."

But she kissed him, curved her arms behind his neck, wrapped her legs around his waist, until all he could say was "Yes!"

* * *

They showered and dressed in time for the boat to dock at the mansion. Marcus wasn't home, but the *Dirty Diana*'s crew knew exactly what to do. Seven and Bailey left the boat with their small bags and drove directly to his place. Although it was only a few blocks from her condo, it was closer. They tumbled into the large apartment, mouths and hips joined, their honeymoon uninterrupted. It felt good to have her in his place. It felt good to have her. He hadn't realized just how much he'd wanted her until she had asked to be in a relationship. With the burden of uncertainty gone, leaving him light and unencumbered, he realized how heavy it had been, how much he had worried. And now, she was his.

Because of this, it was important to him that they come to a place that also belonged to him in some way. They'd spent most of the week on Marcus's boat and a few days at his parents' house. They'd made love, they'd fought, they'd laughed, but none of it had seemed real until they'd come back here. He liked the thought of her surrounded by his things. Seven kissed her harder and she gasped in pleasure, sinking her nails into his shoulder, tearing away his shirt.

"Take me to your bed," she said.

And because he always gave a lady what she wanted, Seven did just that.

The sun slanted gold through the high glass windows and across her naked back. She was so beautiful and fierce. It humbled him that she'd chosen him. They had made love into the evening and talked tentatively of a future. He could see, even in the middle of those conversations, that there was a waiting in her, a sense of another shoe dropping not too far away. But she had stayed with him through the night, past the lovemaking, past the conversations that left them delirious with hope for what the two of them could be.

Monday morning. Sunlight poured into the room even more, molten on her skin and the dark sheets of his bed. It was nearly eight o' clock and time for her to leave for work. She lay in his bed as if she belonged in it, sprawled on the half she immediately claimed after they'd untangled themselves that last time. He didn't want to wake her, he didn't want her to leave, but he knew that soon enough, she had to go.

He looked up as his cell phone rang. Bailey made a sleepy noise and rolled over, and the sun followed her movement in the bed, gilding her beautiful brown body, framing her breasts, the rise of ribs, her flat stomach. The phone rang again. Reluctantly, Seven reached over to the bedside table and picked it up.

"Hello?"

"Seven, I've been trying to reach you damn near all week." His agent's voice leaped at him through the phone.

"Now you've reached me, what's up?"

Neville made a sound of exasperation. "The Rio commission. You got it."

"What?" He sat up in the bed. "Are you serious?" A smile split his face.

"Would I be calling you at this hour to play games?"

"Damn, that's good news!"

"It's bloody great news, Seven. You need to get your ass down here and sign the papers so they can send us that first big check."

"Email it to me. I'll sign it and scan you a copy." He shook his head. "Damn, I can't believe Rio wants me." It was a commission of a lifetime. A piece of art in one of the most dynamic and beautiful places in the world.

Nearly a million dollars for the project, even factoring in Neville's share.

"However you do it, just get the paperwork to me. I'm sending it to you now."

"Okay, cool!" Seven hung up the phone, amazed.

Beside him, Bailey sat up. She yawned and rubbed her eyes. "Good news?"

"The best." Naked, Seven got up from the bed. He was energized, pumped, barely knowing what to do with himself. "I just got offered a commission in Rio. A big, big deal. Lots of money. It would take my career to the next level."

Bailey froze in the bed. "But I thought your career was already up there."

"It is, but when it's possible to go higher, you go for it."

"Does that mean you have to go? Go to Rio." Her voice was tentative.

"Yes, but only for a little while." He saw the look on her face. "I have to go. This is the chance of a lifetime."

"Of course it is." She sounded tired and sad at once. "Do you say that every time you get one of these? Is that the one you can't do without?"

She didn't wait for him to answer. Wearily, she lifted her body from his bed as if it weighed a thousand pounds. "Go," she said. "Go to Rio, then. But don't expect me to be here waiting when or if you get back." She grabbed the few bits of clothes she had strewn around the bedroom and stalked out to the living room, where she'd left her overnight bag.

"You could come with me." Seven followed her, his hands held out in supplication.

"I already wasted a whole week with you and probably lost all chances to be partner because of it."

He flinched as if she'd slapped him. *Wasted?*

Bailey yanked on her jeans and T-shirt, stuffed her feet into black sandals, her hair wild around her head. "Why would I pick up my life here and follow you and your dreams halfway across the world?" She shook her head and sneered. "Negro, please."

"Bailey—" Seven stopped. He didn't know what to say.

She flung open his front door. "Enjoy Rio and have a nice life." The door slammed behind her with the sound of a death drum.

Chapter 26

Inside she was numb. Seven's words and the events of the past few hours and days flooded through her mind like a far-gone dream. She shivered. What she'd always feared about becoming involved with a man like Seven, with Seven himself, had become a reality.

He was leaving for Rio. Not anything small-time like her parents had chased all their lives; something big and prosperous that suited the larger-than-life existence he had. But it was still inconstancy. It was still a ship on a storm-tossed sea, vulnerable to pirates and sea monsters and strikes of lightning.

Bailey left Seven's condo and drove the few blocks to her own, fumbled with the keys and opened the door.

"So, how was it?" Bette asked as soon as she walked in.

The TV was on. Her sister lay sprawled on the couch as if she hadn't left it for the whole week's time Bailey was gone.

"It was a mistake."

She dropped the bag on the floor near the door and headed for the kitchen. The entire condo was illuminated with sunlight, mocking her dreary mood. She had to go to work. Bailey opened the fridge and poured herself a glass of orange juice, walked back into the living room and sat next to her sister on the couch.

Bette's eyes scanned her face. "What's wrong?"

"I shouldn't have gone with him."

"I thought he didn't give you a choice." The look on Bette's face said she approved wholeheartedly of Seven's strategy.

"He didn't. But I had a choice about how I reacted on that boat." Bailey sighed heavily, unwilling to say any more about it. "I need to go to work." She moved to get up from the couch, but her sister grabbed her arm.

"Not until you tell me what's wrong."

"He's leaving Miami." She took advantage of her sister's surprise to tug her arm away and head into the bedroom. There, she stripped, showered and got ready for a long day at the office. She called her secretary to let her know she would be coming in and checked if there was anything that needed her urgent attention. When she went back into the living room, her work armor on—high heels, black slacks, a white blouse, her hair parted down the middle and framing her lightly made-up face—her sister shook her head.

"Are you overreacting?"

"No."

"Where is he going?"

Bailey told her about the award and where he was going. Bette looked impressed.

"That's amazing. It's not some mediocre crap, Bailey. That's the real deal. He could write his own ticket after that commission."

"That's what he said."

"Then what's your problem? He's not like our parents. He's successful, he won't go broke waiting for the next big thing."

"But he'll never be stable. He's not what I need."

Bette shook her head again. "What you need and what

you think you should want are two different things, and you're mixing them up, big-time."

"I'm not confused, I'm making a choice."

Bette made a dismissive noise. "Whatever."

"I'm going to work."

Bailey left her sister in the apartment and drove to work.

As she stepped out of the elevator at the office, the receptionist looked up. Her face immediately assumed a mask of condolence.

"I was sorry to hear about your sick aunt, Ms. Hughes. I hope she's much better now."

She knew her face looked strained, so it wasn't farfetched to think she had been holding a vigil for a fictional relative the entire week.

"Thank you, Celeste." She headed down the hall to her office.

Once there, she propped her briefcase in one of her visitor's chairs and sat in her own. Sat staring out at the Miami landscape, her mind carefully blank, hands clasped in her lap. Things had been so perfect. The thought snuck in despite her vigilance, and to her horror, she felt her chin begin to wobble. The backs of her eyes burned.

No. Bailey swallowed. It was for the best. This was for the best. She took a deep breath and pressed her palms to her hot cheeks. Now was not the time to fall apart. She'd been at this place before and she'd recovered. She would again.

But that's not true, a voice at the back of her mind said. She'd never felt like this about any man. Clive was a drop of water compared to the wide sea that was her yearning for Seven. She cleared her throat. It didn't matter. Bailey pressed a button on her office phone.

"Celeste, can you bring me a cup of coffee, please?"

"Yes, Ms. Hughes."

Bailey got to work. Not long into her workday, a knock sounded at her door. She looked up from her computer screen.

"Come in."

Raphael Fernandez and Harry Braithwaite stood in her doorway.

"Do you have a moment, Bailey?"

"Of course. Please sit down." She saved her work on the computer and gave the two partners her complete attention while they each claimed a seat in front of her desk. "Is something wrong?"

"No, not at all." Mr. Braithwaite cleared his throat. "We were both very sorry to hear about your sick aunt. Your sister told us how very close you are to her. My family and I prayed for you this week."

Seven was right. She shouldn't have worried. Bette could sell snow in Antarctica. "Thank you. Everything worked out fine. She's fine. Thank you for your prayers." She waited to see what else they wanted, because she would bet money it wasn't to talk about her ailing relative.

Now it was Raphael's turn to clear his throat. "We wanted to approach you about this last Monday, but you were indisposed."

She clenched her teeth against apologizing for her absence. She was sure Bette had done a much better job of that than she ever could. Bailey clasped her hands on top of her desk and waited.

"Rightly so, of course," Raphael said. "One thing I don't think we stress enough here at the firm is the importance of a work/life balance. For a while, we were worried that you weren't being mindful of that."

"I think the entire eight years you've worked here, you only missed work once," Mr. Braithwaite interrupted.

She'd actually never missed a day, only come in late one day three years ago because she had a dentist appointment that couldn't wait. But Bailey didn't correct them.

Raphael shook his head with impatience. "The point is, we've noticed and appreciate your hard work and dedication to the firm and thought it was time we—"

"Made you partner," Mr. Braithwaite finished with a smile.

Bailey sucked in a disbelieving breath, but otherwise forced herself not to react.

"Will you accept our offer?"

She smiled. "Of course."

"Good." Both men stood up and offered their hands in turn for Bailey to shake.

"Welcome aboard to Braithwaite, Fernandez and Hughes."

His words surprised a wider smile from Bailey. "Thank you. Thank you very much."

"There's a little office gathering after work in celebration of this new change," Raphael said, his eyes twinkling with good humor. "I hope you can make it."

"I'm sure I can."

As soon as they left, Bailey picked up the phone and called her sister, ignoring the brief and sharp impulse to call Seven first.

"They just made me partner," she gushed as soon as Bette answered the phone.

"Seriously? Finally, after all this time?" Her sister laughed softly. "Congratulations, sister!"

"I can barely believe it." Bailey leaned back in her chair, holding on to the hot surge of exhilaration and relief she still felt from the conversation with her bosses. Well, her partners.

"You and me both. Have you signed any papers yet?"

"Later this afternoon, I think."

"Well, you better sign quick before they change their mind."

Bailey smiled. "It won't be like that."

"Ha! Don't trust those corporate types as deep as you can bury them. Get those papers signed and come back to your place so we can celebrate." She heard Bette take a soft breath through the phone. "Are you finally happy, Bailey?"

The question stopped her cold. All morning, she had been working hard to push Seven from her mind. At times she was more successful than others, at times he might as well have been sitting beside her in the office. Bailey had asked Celeste for a cup of hot chocolate, and the taste of it had reminded her of Seven, of the hours she'd spent with his mother in the small Jamaican kitchen.

"I'm happy, Bette." But even to her own ears, she didn't sound convincing.

The party felt as though it could have happened without her. After the office officially closed for the day, the over two dozen employees of the firm gathered in the lobby for champagne, hors d'oeuvres and hummingbird cake. It was a blur of handshakes and well-wishes. The lobby had never been that crowded before. The top of Celeste's desk had been taken over by the cake and fresh glasses of champagne, while the partners, other associates, their secretaries and Celeste happily mingled in the lobby, glad to have a reason to finish work early and drink champagne on the firm's tab.

"Congratulations, Ms. Hughes," Celeste said in her faint Bahamian accent. "You deserve this." The receptionist stood nearly as tall as Bailey in her stilettos, her clothes elegant and immaculate as always, even at four-thirty in the afternoon.

Bailey thanked the woman, squeezed her arm, then continued on to the next well-wisher. She should be happier. Instead, she was fighting to keep the smile on her lips as she moved through the cool lobby, fighting to keep her mind away from Seven and her sister's words.

There are better things out there than work.

She didn't disagree, but why did she have to choose between work and these other things? She was enough of a woman to want love and a husband to share her life with, but she was enough of a feminist not to want to sacrifice her job for that relationship. Her eyes swept around the lobby, at the people enjoying themselves, celebrating her success. They laughed and toasted, ate cake and hors d'oeuvres. She didn't even have to be there. Her ambivalence about the promotion was irritating. This was what she'd worked for and wanted for eight years. She should be dancing on the desks, celebrating with her whole heart.

Instead, she thought about Seven and the last time she'd seen him. The happiness draining from his face. His hurt look as she'd slammed the door and left the condo. It destroyed her to see him like that. But she refused to give up her dream of a settled life for an uncertainty.

Although a few of the associates wanted to go out to a bar afterward and continue the celebration, Bailey headed home.

She stepped into the condo to see her sister in the exact place she'd left her earlier that day, sprawled on the couch, this time wearing black leggings and a T-shirt advertising some art colony in upstate New York. A bucket holding a bottle of champagne was on the table, next to a box from a local pizza parlor. Bette put her cell phone down as Bailey walked into the door.

"Hey, big shot." She jumped up from the sofa to clasp Bailey in a warm congratulatory hug. "Good job, baby sis."

She tugged the briefcase from Bailey's hand and dragged

her over to the couch. "Sit. Let me pour you a drink." Bette popped the champagne and poured them both a glass. "And eat some of that pizza. I'm sure you haven't had anything all day."

Bailey sighed. "I meant to eat, but all I had was some hot chocolate and coffee." And a mandatory slice of cake at the office, along with a half-finished glass of champagne.

"Please eat something," Bette said again. "Being partner doesn't mean you have to deprive yourself."

Bailey looked sharply at her, but her sister's expression was deliberately innocent. "You know, I could get used to living at your place. I walked to the beach this afternoon, and it was so nice not to fight off the weekend crowd or hunt for a place to park." She put a slice of pizza in one of Bailey's hands and a glass of champagne in the other. Bette picked up her own glass and clinked it against Bailey's.

"To your bright future." Bette sipped her champagne and smiled over the rim at her.

Bailey put the flute to her lips, tasted the sweet champagne, which was like the soda she'd had in Jamaica with Seven. She winced at the thought of him, hid it by biting into the slice of pizza.

"So now that you have all this power, when are you going to take over the world?"

Before Bailey could answer, her phone rang. She swallowed the bite of pizza in her mouth, put down the champagne and plucked her phone out of her briefcase. Marcus's smiling face looked up at her from the front of the phone.

"What's going on, Marcus?"

"I'm glad I caught you." Marcus sounded rushed, as though he had been running. "There's been an accident."

Bailey's stomach clenched in sudden worry. "What? What kind of accident?"

"Seven. You need to come see him."

Her hand clenched around the pizza. "Is he okay?"

"Do you have a pen? Take down this address. He's here. Hurry!"

She fumbled for a pen and notebook in her briefcase, wrote down the address. "Hello? Where is this? Is that a hospital? What happened?" But she was talking to empty air. She lowered the phone.

"What's wrong?" Bette looked up at her with curiosity.

"I… Marcus said Seven was in an accident."

Her sister immediately rushed close to Bailey. "Oh, God! Is he okay?"

"I don't know…." She looked around for a moment, swallowed in panic, uncertain about what to do. The slice of pizza dangled from her hand, the cheese swirling among the limp and pale vegetables suddenly making her stomach queasy. Bailey dropped the slice of pizza back into the box.

"He told you where to go?"

"Yes." Bailey trembled with worry.

"Come, let me take you." Bette put down her champagne and grabbed her purse and cell phone. "Let's take my car."

In a daze, Bailey let her sister take the lead. She gave Bette the address and they rushed from the apartment into Bette's green Honda, where they sped through the night to the place Marcus told her. The address led them to the warehouse district. They drove through the lamp-lit streets, passing cars, whipping through traffic at a speed Bailey would have normally cautioned her sister against. Now she wanted her to go faster.

What kind of accident was it? Had they called an ambulance? The useless questions swirled through Bailey's head as they drew closer—as a snail's pace, it seemed—to where Seven lay. Maybe dying. Maybe dead. Oh, God!

"Go faster, Bette! Please."

"If I go any faster I'll kill us before we get there. Chill!"

A few seconds later, the car skidded to halt.

"Is this it?"

It looked like a block of warehouses, low and squat. Some had cars parked out front, but most were empty and dark. There was no ambulance in sight.

"Does no ambulance mean he's already dead?"

"No, don't think that." An indefinable expression crossed her sister's face. "There, there is the address." Bette pointed to one of a dozen nearby buildings. Bailey ran toward it, heart in her throat. Pulse racing.

She shoved open the door and was instantly engulfed in an incredible heat. A wall of power tools blocked her view into the warehouse. She quickly crept along it, calling Seven's name. A sound reached her, metallic, like raindrops hitting a tin roof. The wall of tools abruptly disappeared. Sparks. She saw sparks, and then a tall figure in thick boots, jeans, a long-sleeved shirt and a heavy-looking apron draped over his front. The figure seemed too tall and stocky to be a woman. An iron mask covered the man's face, protected him from the shower of sparks flying up as he melded two large, curving pieces of metal together. Something about the figure was familiar.

"Seven?"

The man stayed focused on his task. Sparks blossomed up from the metal; the sound, almost like sparklers, popped in the room. Bailey called his name louder. The welding stopped. The sparks disappeared. The masked figure turned toward Bailey. He put down the welder and swept off his helmet. It was Seven. Beautifully whole, a film of sweat over his face, a frown between his brows.

"Bailey?" He looked confused but unhurt. Carefully, he stepped from the platform with the cooling pieces of metal and came closer to her. He took off the heavy apron and hung it on a nearby hook. "What are you doing here?"

"I thought— I heard you had an accident." She looked behind her, trying to see her sister. "Bette drove me. Marcus said…" Her voice tapered off. "They tricked me."

His expression cleared. "I'm sorry you drove all the way over here for nothing." He held his arms up from his body, a parody of the crucifixion. "As you can see, I'm in one piece. You can go home now." He stood watching her.

She sagged where she stood. All the way on the drive, she had made all sorts of promises to herself, to God, to her sister's Ifa deities, to let him be okay. If he was okay, she would cherish him. She would keep him close and never let him go. Even with the promotion, she was still unhappy, dissatisfied. With him, there had been no dissatisfaction, only contentment and the certainty that she was adored. Absolutely.

"I was wrong," she said. It felt good to say the words. A relief. "I love you. I'll go to Rio with you if that's what you want."

He looked at her in deep astonishment. "What brought about this change of heart? Just because you thought I was bleeding to death somewhere on the streets?" Seven shook his head. "Well, I'm not. Rest your conscience."

"It's not my conscience that I'm worried about, it's my heart." She clasped her hands in front of her. "I need you in my life, Seven."

He looked at her for a long moment, face carefully blank. "Bailey, I'm an artist. That's never going to change. Do you realize what that means?"

She took a quick, deep breath.

"I got the promotion."

"Oh! Congratulations." A smile of genuine pleasure crossed his face, sweeping aside the earlier blankness. "I know you wanted it for a long time."

"Yes, I have." She blew out a slow breath. "But now that I have it and I stand to lose you, the choice seems simple."

He shook his head, stepped closer. "If you want this, if you want me, there is no choice for you to make. I want to be with you. Rio and everything else can sort themselves out." The scent of sweat and metal rose from his body. He touched her cheek and she smelled the leftover hint of leather from the gloves he had worn. "I love you, woman."

Her heart tripped inside her chest, settled, opened to fully enclose and encompass him. "Why didn't you just say so in the first place?" She snuggled close to him with a sigh.

Seven chuckled softly, leaned down to kiss her. Against her lips, he was warm and vibrant. The perfection she'd always known. Bailey pulled back from him, looking into his slumberous eyes. *This is the man for me.*

"Marry me," she murmured.

Surprise flicked across Seven's face. Then he chuckled again, hands firm and certain on her waist. "I thought you'd never ask."

Bailey smiled up at her man and tilted her mouth to receive his kiss.

* * * * *